"Hi, honey." I knew I sounded like a schoolgirl with a crush.

I couldn't help it. I acted that way every time I heard his voice or got around my fiancé.

"Cici." Audie's suave actor's baritone sounded as fierce as the Emperor's in *Star Wars*. "Come down to the store."

"Why? What's happened?" Audie had a key to my business, of course, but what took him there after hours?

A heartbeat passed before Audie answered. "I saw a light on at your store so I went in to check it out."

"And?"

"There's—there's a dead man on the floor."

Other mysteries by Darlene Franklin

Gunfight at Grace Gulch

Don't miss out on any of our great mysteries. Contact us at the following address for information on our newest releases and club information:

Heartsong Presents—MYSTERIES! Readers' Service
PO Box 721
Uhrichsville, OH 44683
Web site: www.heartsongmysteries.com

Or for faster action, call 1-740-922-7280.

A String of Murders

A Dressed for Death Mystery

Darlene Franklin

HEARTSONG
PRESENTS
MYSTERIES

Dedication
I could not have written the Dressed for Death series without
the enthusiastic support of my Oklahoma connections—my
beloved son and daughter-in-law, Jaran and Shelley Franklin.
Thanks for your loving support and a spare bed whenever I
visit.

ISBN 978-1-60260-140-6

Scripture taken from the HOLY BIBLE, NEW INTERNATIONAL
VERSION®. NIV®. Copyright © 1973, 1978, 1984 by International
Bible Society. Used by permission of Zondervan. All rights reserved.

All of the characters and events in this book are fictitious. Any
resemblance to actual persons, living or dead, or to actual events is
purely coincidental.

Cover design: Kirk DouPonce, DogEared Design
Cover illustration: Jody Williams

*Our mission is to publish and distribute inspirational products offering
exceptional value and biblical encouragement to the masses.*

Printed in the U.S.A.

From: Elsie Holland (Snoozeulose@ggcc.com)
Date: Friday, April 18, 9:35 PM
To: Jessie Gaynor (Gaynor_Goodies@ggcoc.net)
Subject: Inheritance?

A recent edition of the Grace Gulch Herald
*reported that "Jessie Gaynor has returned to Grace
Gulch to take over operation of local institution,
Gaynor Goodies."*

*I have information that suggests there was more
behind your return to Grace Gulch than family
feeling.*

*Expect further communication from me on the
subject.*

Saturday, April 19

One advantage of dresses from the '30s is the low back,
especially when you zip them by yourself. Not that
I would need to worry about zipping tricky zippers by
myself for long, thank you very much. I still want to pinch
myself every time I look at the European-cut diamond my
fiancé, Audie Howe, gave me last Christmas.

Let me introduce myself. I'm Cecilia Wilde, middle
child of the three Wilde sisters and proprietress of Cici's

Vintage Clothing in Grace Gulch, Oklahoma. I dress in outfits from my store, like the '30s number I have on today, for a variety of reasons. Advertising comes to mind first, but it's also fun. I spent years pretending to be someone else. Thanks to Audie, I had finally accepted my dandelion-seed hair, as well as my eccentricities—like dressing in costume.

I twirled in front of a full-length mirror, admiring the slim line fit that flattered my figure and froufrou sleeves that fluttered around my shoulders. A perfect spring dress for a beautiful spring day. I might even turn some heads when I walked into Gaynor Goodies this morning.

Stop kidding yourself. Only strangers unused to my habit of wearing vintage clothing would stare at me. A stop for some baked pastries had been a part of my daily ritual ever since I opened my store back in 2003. I picked up a clutch purse—barely big enough for my keys and wallet—and headed out the door to the turquoise Civic waiting in my driveway.

As expected, most of the cars in Grace Gulch's five-block business district clustered around the entrance to Gaynor Goodies. Jessie had taken over the business from her elderly aunt early in the year. She added to its already robust success by opening half an hour earlier, setting up free Internet access for paying customers, and oh, yes— increasing the bakery's status as gossip central.

No one could keep a secret for long in Grace Gulch.

The clock read twenty minutes to nine when I walked through the door. Instead of the usual bustle at the counter, most of the customers clustered around Jessie at one of the monitors.

Jessie Gaynor was a living example of the quality of

her products. Her broad face beamed with laughter under gray-streaked brown hair kept under a sensible net. She looked like a sugar confection herself, dressed today in a candy-striped pink-and-white apron, her lip color a frosted pink leftover from an earlier era. Audie and I had secured her services to bake our wedding cake.

"Can you believe that?" Jessie's girlish laugh, more appropriate for someone my sister Dina's age than a middle-aged matron, pealed across the room.

"Yes, Jessie, tell us about it." Lauren Packer, one of the town's three lawyers, spoke up. "What really happened to Aunt Edna? Did she retire to sunny Arizona or did you do her in?" He waggled his dark eyebrows over the pointed nose and chin that had earned him the nickname "vulture." His abrasive personality and occasional ambulance-chaser tactics didn't help either. Only his position as the attorney of one of Grace Gulch's leading citizens, Magda Grace Mallory, saved him from general disdain.

I looked out the window at the brilliant spring sun. On a day like today, it was hard to imagine anyone wanting to move away.

Jessie laughed again. Then she looked up and noticed me for the first time.

"Sorry, folks! I've got customers to take care of." She hefted her body off the chair and walked behind the display cases. "Good morning, Cici. If it's Saturday, you must want some of my frosted sugar cookies."

Jessie knew my weakness. I used the excuse of the many children who visited my store on weekends to buy the overly sweet cookies. But I always saved one or two for myself.

"I'll take two dozen, please. A variety."

She picked up cookies between sheets of waxed paper and packed them in a bakery box. I was curious about the fuss, but I wouldn't ask. I didn't need to. Jessie couldn't avoid sharing a good bit of gossip.

I wasn't disappointed.

"I received a *most* interesting e-mail when I checked my account this morning."

Lauren joined us. "Someone practically accused Jessie of ulterior motives in returning home and taking over the business." He stood beside me, pressing the coffee urn for a refill. "I don't believe a word of it, but keep me in mind if this Elsie person writes again. That's close to slander, if you want to pursue it."

Vulture, I thought.

"I'm sure that won't be necessary." Jessie gave me change. "I don't even know who Elsie is."

Lauren took his cup of fresh coffee and headed for the exit. The bell on the door jingled as he left, and I was ready with my question.

"Who sent it?" I confess I enjoy a bit of gossip as much as the next person. That is, as long as it isn't about me.

"Someone named Elsie Holland. None of us have heard of her."

"Me neither."

"Elsie Holland?" A familiar voice repeated the name.

Audie. My fiancé walked up to the counter and kissed me on the cheek. "Good morning. Don't you look nice today."

I could have stood there all day, drinking in the admiration shining in his dark blue eyes. I was glad to see him in good spirits today. Lately moodiness often darkened his countenance.

"Do you know an Elsie Holland?" Jessie's brows shot upward.

No wonder Jessie sounded surprised. How could Audie, a recent addition to our community, know someone she didn't?

"It's the name of a character in one of those Miss Marple stories. An innocent young housemaid or something like that." He made his purchase—a plain bagel with black coffee—then snapped his fingers. "*The Moving Finger*. That was the story. All about blackmail and murder."

"Blackmail?" Jessie and I repeated the word at the same time.

She insisted on showing us the strange e-mail she had received, which read: *I have information that suggests there was more behind your return to Grace Gulch than family feeling.*

Seeing the words in black and white made me shiver. Not at all nice. I had never come across anything like it in my quiet little town.

Usually quiet, that is, if I discounted the murder that happened last fall, when the editor of the *Grace Gulch Herald* was killed during Land Run Days.

"Ggcc.com. That sounds like your e-mail address, Cici." Audie's thoughts had taken a different direction.

I shook my head. "No, mine is the same as Jessie's address. Ggcoc.net, for Grace Gulch Chamber of Commerce." I studied the e-mail again. "You're right, though, it does seem familiar. Grace Gulch. . .but what do the last two letters stand for?"

"And Elsie Holland?" This time Jessie voiced the question.

"My guess is that she doesn't exist." Audie nibbled on

his bagel. "At least not under that name. It could even be a man. Young, middle-aged, old. 'The old believe everything, the middle-aged suspect everything, the young know everything.'" He loved to quote Oscar Wilde.

The hand on the clock crept closer to nine.

"I'd better run. I might just make it to my store on time." I smiled at Audie. "See you later?"

"Count on it."

Audie did pop by the store in the middle of the afternoon to explain he wouldn't come over to my house that night.

"Something's come up. I'm sure you understand."

"That's fine," I assured him. It was probably something to do with the next production at the Magda Grace Mallory theater—the MGM for short. A little more than a year ago, Magda Mallory had hired Audie from Chicago to direct the new facility. We met during their first production; my sister, Dina, managed their props and she recommended that I provide costumes. The rest, as they say, was history. This spring he was directing the classic comedy, *Arsenic and Old Lace*.

After work I dropped off the day's deposit and returned to my empty house to study my Sunday school lesson. I started to change into comfortable clothes for the evening, but before I removed my dress, I pirouetted in front of my full-length mirror, imagining a '30s-style wedding dress. It might work. I hadn't decided on a bridal gown yet.

A few minutes after seven, Audie phoned with a quick hello, but didn't explain why he couldn't visit with me. While I baked a pie for tomorrow's family dinner, I flipped through the television channels but didn't find anything interesting. I decided to call it a night and slipped into a comfy nightshirt adorned with smiling cows. My finger was sliding into the center of my Bible when the telephone rang. Bother. I hated the shrill sound. Maybe someday I could change the ring of my landline like I did for my cell phone. I reached over the pillows to my night table and looked at the caller ID—Audie.

"Hi, honey." I knew I sounded like a schoolgirl with a crush. I couldn't help it. I acted that way every time I heard his voice or was around my fiancé.

"Cici." Audie's suave actor's baritone sounded as fierce as the Emperor's in *Star Wars*. "Come down to the store."

"Why? What's happened?" Audie had a key to my business, of course, but what took him there after hours?

A heartbeat passed before Audie answered. "I saw a light on at your store so I went in to check it out."

"And?"

"There's—there's a dead man on the floor."

2

From: Jerry Burton (cbtrotter@redbud.net)
Date: Friday, April 18, 9:37 PM
*To: Victor Spencer (Spencer_Cleaning_*
*   Services@ggcoc.net)*
Subject: FYI
Attachments: Lincoln County Burglaries.
GGHerald.com

I know what you're doing. Meet me at Cici's
Vintage Clothing at 8:30 p.m. Saturday night.

Saturday, April 19

A udie ended the phone call. I'm sure he did because
the next thing I knew, I was sitting in my Civic,
dressed in jeans and a T-shirt. It was only five blocks, but
I preferred to drive when I went out at night. Even in
Grace Gulch, Oklahoma, occasional vagrants and juvenile
delinquents made wandering alone after dark a chancy
decision. *Especially with a murderer on the loose.*

It can't be happening again. Last fall Audie's theater
troupe put on a reenactment of the gunfight between
the two founders of Grace Gulch, Bob Grace and
Dick Gaynor. Everything went famously until the man
portraying Dick Gaynor—Penn Hardy—was actually
shot dead during the fateful scene. We went through a
tense few days when the police homed in on two suspects:

my sister, Dina, because she handled the fatal prop gun and my old boyfriend, Cord Grace, because he fired the weapon. I nosed around and uncovered the real killer.

At least some good came out of that experience. By the time the police caught the killer, I had made up my mind between Audie and Cord. When Audie proposed at Christmastime, I accepted, and we planned to marry in June.

Thoughts of the wedding kept worries about Audie's discovery at bay until I arrived. Blue and red lights flashed on top of Grace Gulch's one and only police cruiser, stationed in front of my store. The presence of cops at this time of day would start the town's rumor mill for sure. *Did you hear what happened at Cici's store last night? Well, she's in trouble again. No telling what those Wilde girls will get up to next.*

Speaking of the police, why hadn't they called me? I turned off the engine and sat immobile behind the wheel, struggling with the implications of a dead man in my store. Audie dashed out to the car and opened the door for me. "Good, you're here. Chief Reiner wants to speak with you."

I groaned at the mention of my least favorite policeman.

"Cici Wilde." Ted Reiner's loud voice matched his size, his chest straining against the polished uniform buttons. Like a beefy Teddy Roosevelt, he bellowed orders in a bullhorn voice. Behind him, Frances Waller, one of the town's four-person police force, wiggled her fingers in greeting. They wore matching solemn expressions.

I swung my legs out the door and stood up, taking in the damage to the store window for the first time. The glass had shattered, shards standing up like ill-formed stalagmites in a dark cave. The elegant Antiqua lettering I had ordered in honor of Oklahoma's recent centennial lay in slivers on the ground. The capital *V* from the word VINTAGE dangled like a precarious icicle. Papers and dresses scattered across the sidewalk.

"Oh no!" I darted forward. "The articles about Bonnie and Clyde. . ." Perhaps that sounded like a silly thing to worry about, but original newspaper clippings from the '30s were hard to come by. And what about the guaranteed-worn-by-Bonnie-Parker dress? I stopped to survey the damage.

"Cici." Frances spoke this time.

I waited for her to say more. I'd rather hear bad news from the younger officer. When she didn't continue, my heart raced. "I know there's a dead body here," I blurted.

Frances looked at Reiner, the two of them silently debating their next course of action. She shrugged, giving in to her senior officer. "You're right. Come this way. We want you to take a look at the body."

"Who is it?"

"We're hoping you can tell us that," Frances said.

"It's—" Audie spoke.

"Hold your comments, please, until Cici has seen the body," Reiner interrupted.

I nodded my agreement. Audie slipped his hand over mine, entwining my fingers with his strong ones. We followed Frances into the darkened store. A pale light emanated from somewhere near the cash register, enough to keep me from stumbling, but it didn't provide enough illumination to reveal the state of the showroom. I reached out my hand to flip on the light switch.

"Stop!" Reiner must have seen me. "We haven't dusted for fingerprints."

I wanted to growl. Reiner loved to throw his weight around. They would find my fingerprints, in any case. After all, it *was* my store.

Audie squeezed my hand, reassuring me. I relaxed, grateful for his presence. I didn't have to face something like this alone, whatever it was.

"We'll need you to check for any missing inventory," Frances said. "Later."

Trailing the officer, I weaved through dresses, brushing against rustling satin and soft cotton. Stylish evening wear, all from the '30s, framed the entrance. Beyond them, other racks and shelves loomed. Shadowy shapes reassured me that the showroom hadn't been stripped.

Sketchy light made my store, as familiar to me as my own bedroom, into a house of horrors. Something else was at work here. The farther we walked into the store, the more an out-of-place odor assaulted my nostrils.

Frances stopped when we reached my cash register. One of those big, box-shaped flashlights splashed a small circle of light in front.

That's when I saw him—a man, neither young nor old, dressed all in black. An ominous stillness surrounded him, the same stillness I had felt when I first saw Penn's body last September. In his right hand, the dead man held a strand of pearls. I sucked in my breath.

"Don't worry, I've got you." Audie's hand on my elbow steadied me.

"Well, well, Cici, look what we have here." Reiner plodded along behind us, his heavy footfalls thudding on the carpet. "A dead body shows up in your showroom."

Audie's fingernails dug into my elbow so hard that I

yelped. Better than the angry retort I wanted to utter, I guess.

"You in there, Reiner?" Dr. Barber, Grace Gulch's on-call pathologist, had arrived. "It's dark in here." Before either officer could protest, he flicked on the overhead light.

Beside me Frances muttered a protest.

The dead man looked much worse in full light. Something, some*one*, had caved in this guy's head. I gagged. Audie grabbed the chair that I keep by the dressing room and made me sit down. I leaned forward and rested my head on my hands, fighting waves of nausea.

"I'll get you some tea." Audie disappeared behind the door to my office where I keep a microwave and small fridge. Reiner followed him, probably to make sure he didn't destroy any evidence.

"Do you recognize him?" Frances's soft voice penetrated my stupor.

I opened one eye and looked a second time, trying to control my shaking. This should be easier than seeing Penn's body last year, because then I knew the victim. This man was a total stranger.

Or was he? Something about him tugged at my memory. If I could see him walk or gesture—

But he would never again move. Nothing short of the last resurrection would ever bring him back to life.

"I'm not sure. I don't know him, but. . .I may have seen him around."

Frances moved aside so that I could look more closely. I took a deep breath, swallowed, and edged my chair forward. More details registered. A few strands of gray streaked his hair. Maybe early forties? Eye color?

Undetermined, clouded as they were by death. His clothes, standard intruder black. His hands, roughened by work, clutched Magda Mallory's beautiful pearls.

Nausea welled up in me again and burned my throat. Tears wet my face. I managed to croak out the fact I couldn't identify him.

"Cici?" Audie knelt beside me, the mug of tea set to one side. His arms surrounded me, shielding me from the dreadful sight. I would never look at the practical carpet the same way again. Wood floor, I thought distractedly. I would have the original wood floor uncovered and restored.

Dr. Barber moved in my direction. I saw his rubber-covered hands and shivered. Noting my reaction, he removed the gloves. He placed cool fingers on my forehead and urged me to lean forward again. "I see you made tea, young man," he said to Audie. "Plenty of sugar?"

Audie nodded.

"Drink it up," the doctor said. I did as I was told.

"Now why don't the two of you go into your office back there." He started to lead us to the small room.

Reiner came out from the office. "All clear, Dr. Barber." He nodded at the newcomer.

"Come this way." Dr. Barber followed us into the office and dug out the not-quite-empty box of sugar cookies. "Eat one." He kept his body between me and the—thing—on my floor and managed small talk about safe subjects, like the wedding and spring planting, my father's plans for the ranch.

The grandfather clock situated beside the register chimed the quarter hour. Only thirty minutes had passed since I arrived at the store. I used a damp washcloth that Audie supplied to freshen my face and took a deep breath.

"Feeling better now? Good. We'll let you know when we're done." Dr. Barber slipped back into the store.

Audie turned my radio on low. Neither of us spoke for a few minutes. The noise of my teeth crunching on another cookie covered sounds from the other room.

"I've done all I need to do here," Dr. Barber spoke, and Audie turned down the volume of the radio. "I'll do the autopsy in the morning, although the head trauma leaves little doubt as to the cause of death."

"When do you estimate—" Reiner barked.

"Time of death? You know better than to ask me that. I'll have your answer after the autopsy."

The front doorbell rang. Feet padded across the floor, followed by rolling wheels—a gurney. The hearse must have arrived. Dr. Barber came in to say farewell and left. For a moment I felt as abandoned as a child lost at a county fair. Then I looked around the office—my domain. Someone had committed murder at my place of business. Anger surged through me, and I stood up in the wake of the energy it gave me. Now that the body had been removed, another concern arose. Had any of my merchandise been damaged or stolen?

I paused before I went into the back room. "Is it okay if I check my stock?"

"Give us a few more minutes. We need to finish our crime scene check." Frances sounded brisk, professional.

I dropped back into my office chair and turned on the radio again. A show featuring classic country songs played in the late evening hours. The wailing tunes turned my stomach, and I flicked off the dial.

Audie held my hand, but his gaze focused on a spot on the wall. I wondered what occupied his thoughts. Lately he had seemed preoccupied much of the time.

Frances stuck her head in the office. "You can go into the back now. Can you check your inventory while you're at it?"

"Of course."

Audie joined me in the back room, away from the mess in front of the cash register. I couldn't understand why the intruder had smashed my lovely front window when he could have forced my back door open without much effort. The chain swung loose from its mooring although the door was locked. The murderer might have exited out the back. I opened the door and looked at the alley. I don't know what I expected to see. Muddy tire tracks left on the asphalt? I should leave the forensics to the police. Even Reiner knew more about it than I did.

I walked through racks of plastic-wrapped merchandise. The most valuable and fragile pieces stayed in the back room. I brought them out when a customer sought a particular item, or sold them via the Internet. Everything seemed in order.

"Cici, come here." Frances called me to my office where she had opened my desk drawers. "We need to ask you a few questions."

At those ominous words, I gave brief thought to contacting my lawyer, Georgia Hafferty. But why should I? I didn't have anything to hide.

"When did you leave the store this evening?"

I relaxed. I'm not sure what I had expected. *Did you murder that man?*

"About quarter past five. I close an hour early on Saturdays."

"And everything was normal when you left?"

I nodded.

"Please talk us through your usual routine when you leave."

"I can show you." I extracted a clipboard from the middle drawer. "Here are the instructions for when someone else closes up shop for me." Tidying up, a quick cleaning, cashing out. . .everyday, normal activities.

"We'll take a copy of this." Frances unclipped the page and added it to her file. "And where did you go after you locked up?"

"Home."

"Can anyone verify that?" Frances glanced at Audie.

"Not unless you count my Bible. I was studying my Sunday school lesson."

Frances might wonder where my fiancé was while I stayed at home alone on a Saturday night, but she didn't ask. They would probably grill Audie at a later time.

"Can you tell if anything is missing? Is the right amount of money in the petty cash box?"

I had already checked. It matched the amount I scratched on my memo pad, right next to the note *Call caterer!* stenciled with curlicues of spring flowers. Right now wedding plans seemed as foreign as the Amazon rain forest. "The money's all here. I haven't checked my inventory yet."

I walked to the doorway and paused, shivering. I couldn't bring myself to enter the front room.

"We can come back tomorrow. You don't have to do this tonight." Audie grabbed my favorite boa, a chinchilla fur, from the back of my desk chair and wrapped it around my shoulders.

"No. I can do this." I walked through the door, grateful that the odor had lessened with the removal of the body. Where was the familiar, welcome scent of sachets and coffee and spring flowers? I wanted to cry again over the devastation wrought on my beautiful, much-loved place of business. The man's life held much more value, of course—the price of a sparrow and all that—but I had invested my life and heart in this place. It reflected me, someone apart from the middle Wilde daughter, the good child who stayed home.

I hiccuped, swallowing a sob, and walked up and down the racks. Nothing seemed out of place. Around the final corner, I approached the cash register again. Magda's pearls now dangled from Reiner's hand.

"You're not taking the necklace, are you?" I squeaked. "It's a gift from Mrs. Mallory."

Reiner glared at me. As a descendant of Dick Gaynor, he did not hold the descendants of the rival Graces in high regard. But he recognized the need to bow to Magda Grace Mallory's position in our small town.

Frances removed the pearls from Reiner's palm and dropped them into an evidence bag. "Sorry. They're evidence in the case. They need to be processed."

"Just. . .be careful with them, please? Mrs. Mallory had them restrung especially for use in the new play." She had neatly bartered the necklace in exchange for a role in the production—Abby Brewster in *Arsenic and Old Lace*. Audie gladly obliged his patron. She won the role on her own merits. She could act and paired well with ensemble regular, Suzanne Jay, as the murdering spinster sisters.

Her promise to donate the necklace to my store after the play's run added incentive. I would donate a portion of the proceeds back to the theater, of course.

Reiner lifted the pearls from the evidence bag and tugged a bit at the string, as if something had caught there.

"Be careful!" The words spilled out of my mouth without thought.

"Yup, we need to check these out." Reiner dropped the pearls back in the bag. "Don't worry, the string is plenty strong. Nothing will happen to your precious necklace."

They continued combing the store for evidence. I disappeared into my office for another cup of sweet tea. I doubted I would get to sleep that night, but the sugar helped stop the shaking. Maybe another cookie?

Audie dabbed his finger into the now-empty box, catching one last smidgeon of icing. He saw my look and grimaced. "Sorry." The word encompassed a wealth of meaning. Sorry for eating the last cookie? For canceling our plans for the evening? For going into the store instead of calling the police? Why had this dear man been so foolish as to try to interrupt a robbery in progress? Anger and worry flooded through me in equal measure.

"You could have been killed. Like that poor man." Tears welled in my eyes again at his brush with danger. "What if you came in while the murderer was still here?"

"Shh, there now." Audie stood behind me and rubbed my back. "I couldn't let someone rob your store." His normally gentle massage attacked my muscles in angry circles, betraying his gentle tone.

"Ouch!"

He stopped the movement and left his hands on my shoulders. "I didn't see anything. Just the light. If anyone was here, they ran out the back when I came in the front door."

"That's what I guessed when I checked the storeroom." I leaned against his comforting arms and closed my eyes. My thoughts gathered together, quilted by the Holy Spirit into a prayer. *Father, what an awful night it's been. I'm scared. Someone came to my store with murder on his mind.*

3

From: Elsie Holland (Snoozeulose@ggcc.com)
Date: Saturday, April 19, 9:35 PM
To: Audwin Howe (AHowe_MGM@ggcoc.net)
Subject: Secrets?

Why are you canceling dinner dates with the charming Cici Wilde? How are you spending all those hours? With whom? Where?

Expect further communication from me on the subject.

Saturday, April 19

Frances appeared in the doorway. "We're finished out here. We'd like to talk to you again." Her gaze swept over both of us. "Come this way, please."

It felt funny to receive an invitation to enter my own store. The corners of Audie's mouth twitched, as if the same thought crossed his mind. He took my hand and we followed Frances to the area in front of the dressing rooms.

"We have just a few questions, a formality."

That sounded a bit like Columbo on the scent of the murderer. Did Frances mean her statement as encouragement or warning? Maybe it was time to call my lawyer. *No,* I decided again.

"Was anything missing from the store when you checked just now?" Her pen poised over a notebook.

I shook my head. "Nothing obvious. I'll have to check against the inventory list on my home computer." I had updated it only last weekend, a blessing in light of the present circumstances.

Reiner lifted something sealed in an evidence bag—a piece of paper. But why? I doubted that the murderer had left a signed confession. The chief held it where I could read it through the plastic. Plain white paper, a computer printout of some kind. Audie and I leaned closer to read the words of the message. Its single paragraph grabbed me by the throat.

I know what you're doing. Meet me at Cici's Vintage Clothing at 8:30 p.m. Saturday night.

My mind whirled. *Who on earth—*

"Did you send this message, Cici?"

Reiner's eyes bored into me, their accusation plain.

Not only murder. Blackmail.

Reiner's unspoken accusation broke my trance.

"Of course not." I snapped my mouth shut and stared at the paper, committing the contents to memory. "That's a stupid question. I'm not. . ." I looked at the page again. "Jerry Burton."

First Elsie Holland on the strange e-mail that Jessie Gaynor received, and now Jerry Burton. Had Jessie told the chief about the threat, since they were related and all?

"How about you, Mr. Howe?" Reiner's glare increased in intensity as he stared at my fiancé.

Audie folded in on himself, a trait I noticed when he puzzled through a problem. My heart went out to him. *Come on, sweetheart, give us one of those great Oscar Wilde quotes you love so much.*

"'One can survive everything, nowadays, except death,'" he said more to himself than to anyone else.

I relaxed. As long as Audie could remember Wilde, everything was right in his world. Trust him to have a good quip for unexpected death.

Reiner didn't appreciate the humor. He repeated his question. "Did you send this e-mail, Audie?"

"What?" Audie frowned. "No. Of course not. You have heard about the e-mails circulating from 'Elsie Holland'?"

Reiner waited for him to expand.

"Jessie Gaynor." I supplied one name. "But who's the other one?"

Audie hesitated. "I received one. It was in my inbox when I turned on my computer at work today. From this same Elsie Holland person, whoever she is." He explained his theory about the alias to the chief.

"You could have written an e-mail to yourself." Reiner blew through his Teddy Roosevelt mustache. "But right now we want to track down Jerry Burton." Again he questioned Audie with his eyes.

"I think you'll find that Jerry Burton also is an alias. He was the hero in the same book by Agatha Christie that featured Elsie Holland."

Reiner looked like he wanted to dispute Audie's conclusion, but he knew that he was probably right. "We'll have to see the e-mail that Ms. Holland sent to you." He returned to the subject of the message Audie had received.

Audie shook his head. "I deleted it and emptied the trashcan on the computer. It's gone."

"Was it along the same lines? Unspecific accusations?" This time Frances asked the question.

"Yes." He didn't expand. "Was the victim holding that e-mail in his hand? The hand that wasn't holding the pearls?"

Reiner looked at Frances but didn't speak.

"It must have been," I answered Audie's question. "Maybe not in his hands, but somewhere in the store."

"How would you know that?" *Did you put it there yourself?* Reiner's tone implied.

I explained the reasoning behind my guess. "You must have found it here, or you wouldn't be asking about it. And it explains why he came here tonight."

No one said anything, their silence confirming my guess.

The grandfather clock chimed eleven, and my knees wobbled. "Do you mind if I sit down? There are chairs in my office."

"We'll only be a few more minutes." Reiner echoed Frances's earlier promise.

Exasperated, I grabbed the chair Audie had pulled out of the dressing room earlier and sat.

"You came into the store. . .why?" Reiner turned his attention to Audie.

"I was driving down the street, on my way home."

"What time was that?" Frances spoke up, pen poised over her notebook.

"A few minutes after eight. I had stayed late at the MGM working on sets for the play."

"And you came by the store. . .when?"

"Maybe five minutes later."

"Why did you stop? Were you hoping to see Cici?"

Reiner repeated his question.

Audie shook his head. "I knew she wasn't there. I had called her at home before I left the theater." He pulled up a chair from the other dressing room and sat in it backward, dangling his hands in front of him. "I saw a light bouncing around the store. Not the usual night-light Cici leaves on. I stopped to investigate. That's when I saw the broken window. I wanted to check it out."

"You didn't call the police?" Reiner made it sound like a federal offense.

"My only thought was to stop whoever was there from doing damage. Instinct, I guess."

"How did you get in if Cici wasn't there?"

"The door was hanging open. And I have a key."

Reiner grunted while Frances took notes.

"How many people have keys to your store?" She addressed the question to me.

I frowned at that. Someone had broken the front window to get in; why did the keys matter? But I answered the question. "Me. Audie. And I have an extra set that I loan to my sister Dina when she helps out." *Since Audie has a key, he wouldn't need to smash the glass.*

"Can anyone verify your whereabouts between six and eight?" Reiner focused on Audie.

Audie frowned at his fingers, entwined in front of the chair. "I was at the theater alone between seven and eight. I wanted to set up the scene for tomorrow night's rehearsal. I called Cici from the theater. I told you that."

Reiner snorted. "Using your cell phone, I suppose. You could have called from anywhere. Where were you before seven? With Cici?"

Audie paused. "No."

Unease rippled through my heart. Few people could provide an alibi for every minute of each day. But did it make him look suspicious to the police?

Reiner continued grilling Audie about the evening. My mind searched for something to distract me from the horror, and my thoughts wandered to my favorite topic: our wedding. I looked around the store, picturing a full-skirted, white organza gown that came straight out of the '50s. Or perhaps an A-line that would have been at home in the '60s. Fashion was my passion, and I wanted the perfect wedding dress. *So many to choose from*, I thought.

Audie pursued me diligently in the months following our investigation into Penn Hardy's murder last fall. Once I had chosen the theater director over my childhood friend, Cord Grace, Audie relaxed and acted like a giddy schoolboy at times. Flowers every day, occasional chocolates, joining in harvesttime celebrations at the family ranch, singing beneath my bedroom window. . .

Even the usual November doldrums, brought on by shortened days and brown ground, sped by unnoticed in a haze of happiness. On Christmas Eve Audie took me to a special dinner out of town, away from prying eyes. He got down on one knee and popped the question.

"Cecilia Wilde, heart of my heart, love for you has blinded me to all others. Will you do me the honor of becoming my wife?" His face paled, blue eyes blazing and hair glistening from a fresh cut. He could have chosen the greatest love poems of all time, but instead he used his own words, tying my name—which means blind—into his proposal. That touched me more than anything Shakespeare might have written.

I leaned over and tousled his hair with my hand.

Looking straight into his eyes, I said "Yes!" and met his lips in a kiss.

During the eternal ecstasy of that moment, Audie slipped a ring on the fourth finger of my left hand. I looked at it now.

"There's something I should tell you." Audie's voice broke into my reverie. "I'm pretty sure I know who this guy is." He sat straight in his chair, color high in his cheeks.

"Why didn't you say so before?" Reiner's words came out in a huff.

"I tried. You didn't let me." Audie's level voice carried impact. "Anyhow, I'm telling you now. It's Vic Spencer. He recently opened a janitorial service, pretty much a one-man show, but occasionally others help out. Word spread, and it seems everybody uses his services. He just got the contract for the MGM."

Now I remembered where I had seen the victim before. Our paths had crossed at the theater a few times, but we never said anything beyond a casual greeting. He was as invisible as most janitors were, rarely seen—since he worked after hours—and never heard except for his cleaning equipment. However, members of the Grace Gulch Chamber of Commerce praised his services. His clients included private homes as well as businesses.

"Is that Spencer with a *c* or with an *s*?" Frances asked, looking up from her notebook.

"With a *c*, I think. I can check. We have his contract on file at the MGM office."

Frances stared down at her notes. "Vic Spencer. That matches the name on the blackmail note. It sounds familiar, but I don't think I've met him."

In a town the size of Grace Gulch, where everyone knew everyone else and their family's history since the 1891 land run, that could be important.

"I think Lauren Packer recommended him to Mrs. Mallory." Audie mentioned the lawyer who handled Magda Grace Mallory's many interests. "He is also involved in our production of *Arsenic and Old Lace*. You might want to talk with him."

"Don't worry, we'll do that."

I could almost see the cogs in Reiner's brain turn and mesh together. Vic Spencer and Audie Howe, both new to Grace Gulch. One dead, the other one the first to find him. It made a tidy package, one that would keep suspicion away from long-standing citizens.

Reiner's next words confirmed my interpretation of his facial features.

"You know, you can be up front with us, Mr. Howe. You saw the light on in the store. You came to investigate and found Mr. Spencer in the process of a burglary. You struggled—"

"No, no, no!" Audie's face twisted in frustration. "He was dead when I arrived. I already told you."

"Audie," Frances's soft voice interrupted him. "We have to ask. If that's the way it happened, it was self-defense. The law allows you to protect your property."

Of course technically the property belonged to me, not Audie, but I knew what she meant.

"No." Audie repeated his single syllable answer as if saying it again would convince them.

Frances looked through her notes. "You still haven't told us where you were before you went to the theater. What were you doing, say, between five and seven?"

Now Frances was questioning Audie? That hurt. I felt betrayed. Reiner's suspicion did not surprise me. He tended to play the role of bad cop to her good cop. How would my fiancé answer?

Audie stared at his hands, locked together in front of the chair, as if expecting them to answer the question for him.

"Mr. Howe? You can answer the question here. . ."

Audie shook his head, still not speaking. What was wrong with the man? He needed to tell them where he'd been and get this nonsense over with so they could go and check it out. As incensed as their interrogation made me, a part of me understood their need to question and verify.

". . .or we can take you to the station."

"What's wrong with all of you?" Tired of their harassment, I jumped out of my chair. "Why are you going over and over the same ground when you should both be out there. . ." I gestured toward the broken window ". . . chasing whoever really did this?"

A breeze swept through the room from the open window and I shivered. I wrapped my hands in the chinchilla boa and wished I had taken the time to dress properly instead of jumping helter-skelter into a light T-shirt and jeans. Daytime in April might be warm, but the nights remained cool, even cold. A heady spring scent, redolent with dogwood and lilac blossoms, drifted in, accompanied by the trilling of a late-night siskin. The normal, joyous rites of spring did little to lift my mood.

Reiner and Frances exchanged another look.

"We have to know the truth, Cici."

Frances's explanation did nothing to calm my nerves.

From: Elsie Holland (Snoozeulose@ggcc.com)
Date: Friday, April 18, 9:40 PM
To: Frances Waller (FWaller@ggpd.net)
Subject: Disappearance?

You have been missing from your post at the piano at Word of Faith Fellowship and from your normal police beat.

I know what you've been doing during your absences.

Expect further communication from me on the subject.

Saturday, April 19

Audie lifted his head. "Can I speak to you privately, officers?"

His response did nothing to dispel my nerves. He refused to look at me. I wanted to put on one of the lace-up boots that stood on a shelf behind the cash register and stomp my foot. What was he hiding from me?

A surprised look flashed across Reiner's face, and a glint sparkled in his eyes. "Let's go to the office, then."

Audie rolled his shoulders and stood. "Don't worry." He must have sensed my concern. He kissed my cheek before he followed Reiner and Frances into the office. My office. It felt like someone else had taken over my life. My business, anyway. A slow-burning anger replaced my earlier tears. No one had the right to do this. Not to that poor dead man, Spencer, or whatever his name was, and not to *me*.

I couldn't stay still. I grabbed a broom and started sweeping up broken glass. The bottom half of the numeral 3 from ESTABLISHED 2003 dangled from a sliver of glass. Someone had brought in the papers scattered on the front sidewalk while I waited in my office. I appreciated the unexpected kindness. Those Bonnie-and-Clyde articles were irreplaceable.

Could I cover the window with something, in case of rain? I wondered.

I could imagine Reiner's reaction. *Don't touch it!*

Instead I compromised by moving the most delicate clothing items behind the counter, out of harm's way. I grabbed a notepad and started a list.

Number one: Call glazier about replacing the window.

How long would it be before the police would allow me to start repairs? And how long would it take before I could reopen? I would have to ask Frances. No business could afford to close its doors for long. Today I had received a couple of online orders. Maybe I could take care of those and update my computer catalog while I waited.

Moisture-heavy air swept through the broken window. I decided to move the racks of clothing into the back room. Crowded conditions were preferable to rain damage or burglary. The storage room had a separate lock so I could make it secure. I propped the door open and rolled the nearest rack—the one with Madonna rip-offs from the '80s—into the back room. Finding something useful to do kept my worries at bay.

I moved to the next rack—tons of polyester from the '70s—but stopped when the wheels rolled over the white chalk outline of the space where Vic Spencer's body had sprawled. I stared, transfixed, at the bloody spot where his head had lain.

Questions mixed with revulsion swirled around in my head, and I stopped working. The police probably wouldn't want me moving things around in any case. I pulled up the chair from the dressing room and took out a notepad. Maybe writing down facts and questions would get them out of my mind. Better yet, maybe they would shed some light on the situation.

Fact: Vic Spencer died in my store tonight. But could he have died somewhere else?

I looked at the floor and decided against it. Someone followed him inside, hit him on the head, and he fell and bled to death on my floor.

Question: Why was Vic Spencer at my store?

Fact: Vic Spencer had an e-mail asking him to come to my store tonight.

Questions: Who sent it? And why?

Question: Was Spencer's death accidental—wrong place, wrong time? Or was it intentional?

Intentional seemed most likely; after all, someone had sent him the e-mail. If it was intentional, what was the reason behind the murder?

Questions outnumbered the facts. The biggest one was why at my store? No wonder the chief liked Audie as a suspect. He had discovered a robbery in progress and killed the intruder. For them that was the simplest explanation.

Audie, what have you been up to? His recent moodiness weighed on my mind. When I asked him about it, he tweaked my chin and said to let him keep his secrets until the wedding. Since I held on to a few of my own, I let it go.

I flipped the page in my notepad and wrote *Audie's Strange Behavior* at the top. Last week he disappeared for a few days and wouldn't say where he went. He missed a couple of our nightly telephone calls. And other times he got through a conversation without quoting Oscar Wilde. His mind wandered to a place he wouldn't let me visit.

Wait a minute. Did I suspect Audie of murder? *No.* I shook my head. He would never kill someone. But he was hiding something from me. And I knew the police would ferret it out.

I flipped the page back and read over my facts and questions. A sliver of excitement pumped into my veins, warming me against the cool evening air. An investigation drew Audie and me close in the first place. Maybe the same magic would work now to lift Audie out of his current funk.

I returned to my task of moving the clothing racks, careful to steer clear of the spot where Spencer had lain. After all the hard work, I'd need to take another shower before bed. I had taken care of two more racks by the time Reiner exited my office, followed by Frances, and then Audie. They were laughing.

Laughing? While I had worked myself into a frenzy during the past fifteen minutes?

"We'll check what you told us," Frances said. "But you're free to go." She noticed me pushing the rack. "You moved things around."

I bristled. "I started to move some things to the back

room, to make sure they don't get rained on. But I stopped. I do need to protect the merchandise. Can I at least cover the window with a tarp?"

"That's fine," Frances said.

"When can I call someone to fix the window and the floor?" I decided to strike while she seemed agreeable to my efforts to return to business as usual. I reached for the tarp and tacked it into place.

"We should finish up here tonight. You can probably call on Monday. I'll let you know." She glanced at Reiner walking the perimeter of the store, checking for what, I couldn't guess. "You are free to go. I'll give you a call. Oh, and don't tell anybody about the e-mail we found."

I promised and headed out to my car.

"Cici."

At the sound of Audie's voice, I whirled around to face him. A hangdog look clouded his features. I had to know the truth.

"What did you tell the police that you couldn't tell me?"

He blinked, shutters that closed the window to his thoughts. Whatever had happened, he wouldn't tell me. Then he smiled and dug out an Oscar Wilde quote. "'One should always play fairly when one has the winning cards.'"

I fumed. Cards, was it? I guess he didn't want to invite me to join his game. Before I could retort, I tugged my car door open.

Audie caught the door and looked at me over the window. "You don't think I had anything to do with the murder, do you?" He studied me, his blue eyes dulled by fatigue.

"Of course not!"

He smiled at that and came around the door to take me in his arms, his hands rubbing slow circles on my back. My head rested against his shoulder. It felt so good. The light glinted on my engagement ring. I looked at it now, the symbol of our present love and promise of our future. Audie had shared its history with me: the European cut diamond set in an art deco platinum band originally belonged to his great-grandmother. It passed to him and held special meaning for us, a celebration of his heritage and my special interest in all things historical.

I relaxed. Whatever happened, I knew things would be okay between us.

"Don't worry," Audie whispered, his voice a low croon. "We'll figure out who did this. And I'll tell you everything. Soon. It's a good surprise. Really."

When he kissed me, I could believe anything. He drew back, and we stood, hands clasped between us.

"Proverbs says that 'He who covers over an offense promotes love, but whoever repeats the matter separates close friends.' Think about that before you go to sleep." Audie kissed me again briefly, and left.

Food for thought. Love, not spite, lay behind Audie's silence.

—

The next morning I slipped on one of my contemporary outfits: a denim skirt and a short-sleeved sweater and added a scarf with spring flowers. I laughed when I looked at my reflection in the mirror. Add a ponytail and I would almost be a poster girl for '50s chic. With a poodle skirt, of course. Even if memories of last night's disaster weighed down my heart, I could at least look cheerful.

I puttered around long enough that I missed Sunday school. I can't say that I was sorry; I didn't want the murder to take the place of the Bible lesson in the adult class. But I did make it to Word of Fellowship in time for the worship service. I was right. News of the previous night's events had preceded me. However, before the vultures could sweep me up for details, Enid Waldberg, the pastor's wife, rescued me. She planted herself by my side.

"Would you sit with me today?" She swept me past the questioning eyes to her usual place near the front. Dear Enid. She was as sweet as her husband was brusque, and they made a good team.

Her request was unexpected; in most churches I had visited, people sat in the same pews week after week, almost as if they were assigned seating. Taking someone else's spot could earn you glares. My family sat in the third row from the back, on the pianist's side. I had been watching Frances Waller play hymns ever since she started at the tender age of eleven.

Frances wasn't at the piano today. I wondered if the investigation had taken her away or if something else had happened.

The investigation. I didn't want to think about it. Instead I listened to soft organ music and studied the new banners hung on Easter Sunday earlier in the month. An empty white cross, a dark crown of thorns, stood on a gold quilted banner. Red silk letters formed the words HE IS RISEN. I sent up a belated prayer for Vic Spencer's family and trusted that whatever his faults, he had gone home to be with the Lord.

Someone called my name, and I glanced over my

shoulder. Dina stood by our usual spot, surprise written on her face. She had recently dyed her short hair bright pink in honor of spring. I waved. The budding reporter would get her chance to question me later.

"Mind if I join you?" Audie looked more handsome than ever in a cadet blue linen jacket and navy slacks.

We slid over in the pew moments before the music director announced the first hymn, "What a Friend We Have in Jesus." The familiar words trickled over me and through me, reassuring me of God's care. The praise team sang "I Am a Friend of God."

Pastor Waldberg preached from John 15: "I have called you friends. . . . " In step with his usual style, he focused on the conditional clause, ". . .if you do what I command."

Every week after church, Audie and I ate dinner at the Crazy W, my family's ranch. We rode together in his Focus. Dina bounded out to greet us. I shook my head. Her pink hair contrasted poorly with the orange T-shirt she had changed into after church. All in all, I preferred the Christmas-red color she sported last fall.

"Come in and tell us all the news! I've been dying to hear all about it."

No surprise, Dina pounced on last night's events.

"And the editor promised I could write an exclusive interview with you about the break-in!"

I smiled at that. Although I didn't want to relive the events of last night, I had expected the questions. I was glad for Dina's opportunity.

She took my sour cream pecan pie from the trunk and ran up the steps. "I'll take care of this. Dinner's ready."

Audie took my hand in his and squeezed it. He seemed to take the Wilde sisters in stride. At least Jenna, my older sister, only came to town for fleeting trips. She was actually Dina's birth mother, but Mom and Dad adopted Dina at birth. The resemblance between my outspoken, outrageous, adorable sisters grew with every passing year. At least in part, I took to wearing vintage clothing to stand out from my two larger-than-life siblings.

A few minutes later, we were seated around the table, crisp salad and sizzling steaks teasing our appetites. Dad opened his Bible and read the verse of the day, something he had done at every dinner I had eaten in this house for as long as I could remember. "He who trusts in himself is a fool, but he who walks in wisdom is kept safe." Dad stared at Audie, his eyes challenging him to identify the reference.

"Proverbs 28:26." Audie came through, as usual. He seemed to have memorized the entire book of Proverbs, as well as most of the works of Oscar Wilde. "That's a good one."

Dad led us in prayer, thanking God for keeping us safe and bringing us together another time. His words triggered thoughts of last night. I was ready to tell the story to my family.

"Stop stalling," Dina said as she handed me a bowl of mashed potatoes. "Spill the beans about the murder."

Audie started the ball going, explaining how he investigated the light in my store and his subsequent discovery of Spencer's body. He kept the description clinical. That didn't matter. Dina had enough imagination to fill in the details and then some.

"I don't know about you, Audie." Dad shook his head. "Ever since my daughter got involved with you, it's been one dead body after another."

5

From: Elsie Holland (Snoozeulose@ggcc.com)
Date: Friday, April 18, 9:38 PM
To: Dina Wilde (DWilde_GGHerald @ggcoc.net)
Subject: Newsworthy?

You recently reported on a string of burglaries
across Lincoln County. You should check your facts
before they appear in print.

Expect further communication from me on the
subject.

Sunday, April 20

Oh, Daddy." I poked him in the arm. "Stop making
fun of my man." One suspicious death last fall, plus
Vic Spencer's, only made two. Of course, that was two
deaths too many.

Audie only smiled. Daddy's ribbing made him feel
like a part of the family.

"Was anything taken from the store?" Dina asked.

"That's the strange thing." I put a pat of butter on my
English peas and watched it melt. "I checked my inventory
list today. The only thing out of place was the pearls."

"Mrs. Mallory's pearls?" As props person for the
play, Dina knew all about the loan. She made the whole
town aware of it when she wrote a piece about it for the

Herald—one of her first articles as their cub reporter. "They're gone?"

"No, but Spencer was clutching them in his hand." I tasted the peas. Dina had cooked them with a hint of onion. Perfect. "Reiner bagged them as evidence." How were we going to explain that to Mrs. Mallory?

"That's curious." Dina started to ask another question.

"Eat." Daddy pointed his finger at my sister. So far she hadn't touched anything on her plate.

Dina forked a bite of salad into her mouth and cut into the steak before she spoke again. "There's been a string of burglaries across Lincoln County over the last few months. Mostly private homes, but some businesses, too. No fingerprints. In every case the burglar only took a few, easily portable things, like Mrs. Mallory's pearls. Very discriminating. Almost like the thief entered the house with a shopping list of the most valuable items." She chewed on the steak and moaned, "Heavenly."

"That's funny." I laid down my steak knife. Audie and I looked at each other before I spoke again. "I assumed he took the pearls as a crime of opportunity."

"You don't think he planned to rob the store?" Excitement flushed Dina's face as pink as her hair.

I grimaced. "I don't know. The guy had an e-mail telling him to meet someone at my store last night."

Dina's hazel eyes opened wide. "What did it say?"

I quoted it word for word. "I know what you're doing. Meet me at Cici's Vintage Clothing at 8:30 p.m. Saturday night."

Dina stopped eating, a piece of steak poised in mid-air. "An e-mail? A threatening e-mail? Do you know who sent it?"

"It said Jerry Burton, but Audie says that's another character in the same book where Elsie Holland appears. Has to be an alias."

Audie coughed. "And he—or she—may have sent more than one e-mail. Jessie Gaynor has received one from 'Elsie', and so have I. Along the same lines."

That news relaxed my sister and she chewed the steak with relish. "'Elsie' sent me an e-mail, too. She accused me of getting the facts wrong when I reported about the burglaries in Lincoln County."

"Aren't you worried?" I was.

"Nah. I know I got my facts straight." Dina paused. "Unless she was involved with the burglaries and she's warning me to stay away from my investigation." Now she looked alarmed.

"So the blackmailer and burglar and killer may all be the same person." I voiced the thought.

"Leave it to the police," Dad said. He didn't want me involved in another murder investigation. "They must have fingerprints and all that stuff."

"They probably won't find any. The guy is careful. He hasn't left any clues so far." Dina's mouth moved around mashed potatoes. "The police told me that when I interviewed them about the burglaries."

"Don't talk with your mouth full." Although Dina was nineteen, I couldn't help it. Mothers, even surrogate ones like me, can't seem to turn it off. I had guided my younger sister ever since our mother died almost fifteen years ago.

I considered what Dina said about the burglar's choosy habits. Was Spencer wearing gloves? I closed my eyes and pictured the hand clutching the pearls—only the hand, not allowing that bloody head to impinge on the delicious dinner. "Spencer had on brown leather gloves. Like a cowboy might wear."

"See. He must be the guy." Dina spoke as if the gloves put the conclusion beyond dispute. "Mystery solved."

"Only there's been a murder," Audie pointed out. He had cleaned his plate and was ready to join the discussion. "I agree with Cici. He showed up at the store for the appointment and couldn't resist the pearls."

The steak turned to ash in my mouth, and I shivered. *Burglary, threatening notes, now murder. What had happened to my quiet little town?* I wished I could turn back the clock and change the history of the past twenty-four hours.

Dina wolfed down the food on her plate and reached for a biscuit. She had a light hand at baking. A punk Julia Child in the kitchen.

"Do we have any clues to the identity of this Elsie Holland person?"

"Well, there's the e-mail address. Her moniker is Snoozeulose, so I assume she's an early bird. The domain was ggcc.net."

"Sounds like the kind of handles we used to use on the radio," Dad said. As usual he finished his meal second, after Audie. "I was the Smokin' Okie." He grinned.

"Ggcc.net? Are you sure that was the address?"

"Pretty sure. Grace Gulch something something."

"Community College. Everyone—students, faculty, staff—has an official e-mail address. And since the server is free, we can create additional addresses if we want to." She buttered her biscuit and added some homemade apple butter. "I have two, myself. One for official school announcements and then a personal one, as well as a few for certain classes and campus groups."

"I should have guessed." I grabbed a biscuit.

"Can anyone outside the school get an e-mail account with the server?" Audie asked. "Alumni, for instance?"

"I don't think so." Dina froze in mid-bite. "That means. . .it's probably someone I know." She was about to graduate with an associate's degree in journalism. The school attracted people from all over Lincoln County, the student body a cross between town and country. After two years she knew almost everyone in the closed community.

"Anyone want more peas?" Dad asked. He wanted Dina and me to finish eating so the men could have dessert. I took a spoonful of potatoes and peas but resisted the lure of more biscuits.

The men cleared the table and stacked the dishwasher while I divided the pie into ample portions—otherwise they'd ask for seconds. Dina made fresh coffee—decaf, to Dad's grumbling disappointment—and we retired to the living room.

"So we have to find out who sent that libelous e-mail." Dina stayed in reporter mode, refusing to let dessert throw her off the scent. "If we can find that out, we know the murderer."

"Not necessarily." I studied the layers in my slice of pie. "The murderer may have sent the e-mail, or it could have been someone else."

"If we knew what the meeting was about, we'd have a better idea." Audie set down his coffee cup, a thoughtful look in his eyes.

"It must have been something shady. Anybody with honest business would go by there in the daytime." Dad grinned at Dina. "When?"

"The five Ws," I said. "Where? My store. But why?"

"Why meet? In secret? At night? At your store?" Dina asked, ticking off the questions while she beat her pen on her steno pad. They echoed my own from the previous evening.

"Maybe Spencer had a partner," Audie speculated.

"But did his partner kill him? Why? Why at my store?" That question bothered me the most. "Somebody lured him to my place of business to kill him. He could have done it anywhere, but they came to my store."

"Or *she*," Audie murmured.

"It's blackmail. Plain as a funnel cloud," Dad said. He put his plate on the floor so our calico cat could lick the crumbs.

"Of course! Yes!" Dina jumped on his suggestion. "All the e-mails state, 'I know what you're doing.'" She made quotation marks with her fingers. "All the e-mails sound threatening."

"Or maybe someone wanted in on the action. Don't they all say, 'Expect further communication from me'?" Audie always could think of an alternate explanation for anything. "A variation on blackmail."

"A rival thief?" Dina suggested. "You're invading my turf."

"As to why your store. . .I think I know the reason for that. The *Herald* ran Dina's piece about Mrs. Mallory's pearls last week. Anyone who reads the paper knows about them. Perfect for our thief. If it is the same man." Audie shook his head. "It's hard to believe Spencer was a thief. He came with excellent references."

"It would be interesting to compare those references

against the robberies," Dina said. "See if there are any matches."

"Oh, no you don't." I jumped into big sister mode again. "Don't go sticking your nose where it doesn't belong and asking for trouble."

"You're a fine one to talk, after being shot at last fall." Dina pointed a forkful of pecans in my direction. "And you're dying to look into this guy's murder. I can tell." She put the pie in her mouth, chewed and swallowed. "All I'm asking is that you allow me to help."

"'Whenever a man does a thoroughly stupid thing, it is always from the noblest motives,'" Audie quoted. "Although I'm not sure if curiosity is a noble motive. And blackmail and greed definitely are not."

The three of us stared at him. It's a wonder that our matching hazel eyes didn't turn him summer brown on the spot.

"Oscar Wilde again?" Dad allowed a glimmer of a smile to lighten his lips.

"Of course. When is Jenna coming to town?" Audie said. Now there was a change of subject if I ever heard one. Or maybe he was dreading the day when he would have to take on all of us at one time again.

"In a couple of weeks." Dina nodded her bright pink head. "I hope you decide on your bridesmaids' dresses soon. It's time to color my hair again, and I want to match." Wedding plans could distract her from almost anything.

For a fleeting second, I considered asking her to let her hair return to its natural, pale blond state. I shook my head. No way. I loved my younger sister, funky hair and all. I loved Jenna, too, although my feelings for her fluctuated between resenting her escape from family responsibilities and adoring her larger-than-life personality.

"I'll decide by the time Jenna gets here, I promise. I have to. Enid wants to get our measurements for the gowns." I winked at Audie. "But I can't talk about it here. It's supposed to be a secret from the groom."

He winked back. "As long as you allow me to keep my secrets until the wedding, as well." His blue eyes bored into mine, the two of us suspended in our own special moment in time. *Trust me*, his eyes said.

I thought about those eyes, as blue as an Oklahoma spring morning, when I got ready for bed that night. I did trust him, but he was comparing pecans to pine nuts. Equating the design of the bridesmaid dresses with his alibi for the time of a murder was ridiculous.

Restlessness surged through me. I grabbed my brush and sat down at my dressing table. Maybe one hundred brushstrokes would settle me down. Not that any amount of brushing kept my hair in order for very long. My hands rubbed the mother-of-pearl finish of the brush. A Christmas present to myself a couple of years ago, the smooth surface soothed my fingertips. I lifted it to the top of my head and gently ran it through my tangled hair.

This should be the time of my life. I'm getting married in two months! But another murder—in my store, no less—increased my already jittery pre-wedding nerves.

And hurricane Jenna—as I privately dubbed my older sister—would descend on Grace Gulch before long. Some memory stirred in the back of my mind. What was it? Jenna, talking about an older bully in school. . .*Spencer*. The murder victim had attended Grace Gulch schools, at least for a few years. Not as much of a newcomer as I had first thought.

I brushed my hair in long, steady strokes. *"My peace I leave with you,"* Jesus promised.

God, I need that peace.

Brushstroke by brushstroke, I calmed down. God would see me—see us—through the latest troubles.

But in the meantime, I had a job to do. I had to find out who chose my store as the place to kill Vic Spencer.

I glanced at my closet door and thought about my ensemble for tomorrow. Maybe I should add my wrinkled trench coat to tomorrow's outfit. Cici Wilde, amateur detective extraordinaire, was back in the detective business.

6

From: Elsie Holland (Snoozeulose@ggcc.com)
Date: Sunday, April 20, 9:35 PM
To: Peppi Lambert (PLambert@ggcc.net)
Subject: Grades

    Your name appeared on the recent dean's list at Grace Gulch Community College.

    Did you really write the essay that gave you an A and earned your internship at the Grace Gulch Herald*?*

    Expect further communication from me on the subject.

Monday, April 21

O f course I didn't get to start detecting right away. The glazier met me at the store early Monday morning and promised to replace the glass on Tuesday. A small victory. Then I walked the floor and wondered what I was going to do about the spot where Spencer's body had lain. Because blood did *not* come out, even when you could no longer see it. I'd seen enough television crime shows to know that.

I debated about whether or not to replace the wood where blood had seeped through the carpet. Maybe it was time to remove the carpet and return to a polished, oaken floor. Add hooked and braided rugs for a vintage feel. Bags of scraps hid in my closet, awaiting this excuse to rediscover the art of braiding a rug. I bet the Internet had some handy hints. I thought again. Probably not. It sounded like too much work, and besides, I could just imagine someone in high heels tripping on the rugs.

I was deep in thought, staring at the computer monitor in my office, when Dina arrived. She often stopped by on Mondays when she didn't have work or school.

"Are you ready to go?"

"Hmm?" I turned away from the illustrated patterns. "Go? Where?"

"To investigate the murder, of course." She grinned and flipped her neon pink hair in the direction of the empty display room. "This place looks so different when it's empty."

I came to the doorway and looked. I had to agree. Sun danced through dust motes that floated in through open windows. With my old-fashioned cash register, my store looked ready to open its doors to guests arriving by horse and buggy for a day in town. Not surprising, since the building had been constructed before statehood. Whatever remodeling I did, I wanted to keep that atmosphere. But I couldn't do all that today and decided to take the day off. Freedom!

"We should let the police do the investigating." I attempted to do the right thing.

Dina looked at me out of the corner of her eye. "When has that ever stopped the Wilde sisters?"

Her comment brought several of our more outrageous escapades to mind—like the time my sisters had dragged me on stage to dance the cancan at last fall's Land Run Days concert. I smiled. "Where shall we start?"

"I thought you would never ask." Dina reached in the pocket of her big shirt—that strange style of shirt so big that two of her could fit in it—and pulled out a thin strip of paper. "I got Spencer's address from the files at the MGM. I thought we could start there."

I debated telling Audie our plans, but decided against it. He might say no. So we locked the back entrance and climbed into my Civic. The drive took only a few minutes, since Grace Gulch was less than a mile from one end to the other. The condos, built at the turn of the millennium, nestled against the side of the hill that formed the gulch.

I parked in front of Spencer's building and studied the facade. The cedar siding blended into the setting nicely. I had considered moving here before I bought my house, but the price was prohibitive. How had Spencer afforded it on a janitor's salary?

"How are we going to get in?" I should have asked the question before.

"Ask the manager?" Dina said hopefully. "I know her from school. She's as worried as we are about what happened. Murder doesn't fit into the image of 'Gracious Living at Grace Gulch Condominiums.'"

I shook my head at that. Getting the key from the manager might be a step above breaking and entering, but not by much. "No. I suspect it's still illegal. We're already in enough trouble if Reiner learns that we're looking into Spencer's death."

"Can we at least peek in the windows?" Dina moved in the direction of Building C where Spencer's unit was located.

"Don't you feel all the eyes looking at us?" I did. Multiply Grace Gulch's penchant for gossip tenfold in an enclosed community like the condos, and that might come close to describing the sense of unease I felt.

"Well then, what bright ideas do you have?" Sometimes Dina treated me like her doddering grandmother instead of her slightly older sister. Okay, a decade older.

"As a matter of fact, I do have an idea. If Spencer was behind the robberies, where did he fence his stuff? I thought we could check with local pawnshops and see if any of them ever did any business with him." I saw a protest forming on Dina's lips and hurried ahead. "You can help by compiling a list of stolen items. They were in the police reports published in the *Herald*, weren't they? And maybe you can find a photo of Spencer somewhere? Find out if he ran an ad for his services in the paper?"

"I'm way ahead of you. Here's the list." Dina was speaking when someone tapped on our car window. We both jumped. A young woman with naturally bright auburn hair waved at us. I knew her. Polly, Penny, Peppi, that was it—Peppi Lambert. She attended college with Dina; maybe she didn't have any classes today either. I knew her from her involvement with the theater. She got to play the romantic interest, opposite Lauren Packer in a surprising turn as Mortimer Brewster—provided she was willing to remove most of the earrings that ran up and down her left lobe.

Dina rolled down her window.

"Hey, Dina, what are you doing in my neck of the woods? Are you thinking about moving here?"

"Maybe." Maybe she'd like to move into her own place, but Dina knew the advantage of free rent at home.

"I didn't know you lived here."

"Yeah, well, I might want to move somewhere else now." Peppi nodded in the direction of Spencer's unit. "That guy who was killed lived here, you know." Her green eyes registered recognition. "Hey, he died in your store!"

Gulp. "That's right. Did you know him?"

"I saw him every now and then. We didn't talk much." Peppi shrugged. "Can I interest you ladies in a cup of coffee?"

"No." I wanted to get going.

"Yes." Dina surprised me. What did she have in mind? She turned to Peppi. "Can you bring me back to Cici's store later?"

We synchronized our watches, like spies in a movie—and planned to meet back at the store at noon.

I took advantage of the time to research pawn shops in the area and ran to Gaynor Goodies for something to eat. Dina would be hungry. At the stroke of noon, Dina waltzed into the store, followed by Peppi. It was a good thing that I had bought an extra croissant.

"I hope you don't mind if Peppi comes along." Dina peeked in the lunch bag. "Hey, great, turkey cranberry, my favorite." She unwrapped the croissant and dove in. "Peppi's interning at the *Herald* this spring. She wants to join us while we investigate. Be another Jane Marple."

Peppi flashed white teeth. "I'm a big Agatha Christie fan."

Perhaps I should have warned Dina not to talk about our plans. I didn't think I needed to. Had word spread through the entire GGCC campus? Well, if so, it was too late to change anything. I put on my best smile and said, "Sure. Why not? And have a croissant before we head out."

We studied the list of stolen items, as well as the ads Spencer ran for his cleaning service—no pictures.

"We checked the morgue, in case we had any kind of photo—no luck." Dina sucked down her drink.

"Too bad." I chewed the last bite of croissant and threw away the wrapper.

"No photograph—a sure sign of guilt." Peppi ate the salad from inside the croissant with a plastic fork. "At least that's what they say on television."

"More likely, he didn't need it for his business." I avoided pictures myself, and that didn't make me guilty. "You're reporters, both of you. How would you describe him?"

"I didn't pay attention." Peppi screwed up her face in concentration. "He was just around, you know?"

I remembered Spencer only too well. All I had to do was close my eyes, and I could picture his body lying on the floor of my store. The memory made me shiver, so I struggled to remember him from the MGM. A few details emerged. Height: five eight or five nine. Weight: a little chunky. Hair color: Salt-and-pepper gray. Between us we came up with a decent description.

The three of us piled into my Civic. Dina opened the passenger side door in the front, then changed her mind and joined Peppi on the backseat. I felt a bit like a chauffeur, but I didn't mind. I could ignore their chatter and let my mind wander. Soak in the April sunshine and the blooming flowers. April had to be one of the prettiest months in Oklahoma. Trees and flowers burst into life again after the long brown winter months, and temperatures didn't climb too high. The investigation gave me an excuse to travel backcountry roads to places I did not ordinarily visit.

By mid-afternoon we had checked the pawnshops closest to Grace Gulch and debated whether or not we should head to the county seat in Chandler. We stopped at a café in Arcadia. I paused by the entrance, checking to see if the owners had added any more license plates to the wall since my last visit. Historical plates and out-of-state samples plastered the exterior by the door; there wasn't room for one more. Did they replace them from time to time?

Minutes later, the three of us were seated at a polished pine booth. We asked for three spoons and one dish of their berry cobbler à la mode.

"No luck so far." Dina's pink hair looked as out of place in the quaint restaurant as snow in July. But given the café's location on Route 66, the server must have seen stranger things. Dina took a bite of the cobbler before she continued. "I guess it was a long shot. Why should anyone remember Spencer?"

Someone had known something about Spencer. The blackmail e-mail sprang to mind, but I didn't want to discuss it in Peppi's presence.

"Unless he came in all the time or they learned he was handling hot merchandise?" Peppi suggested.

"And no one would admit that." *Why would they?*

Dina swallowed her bite of cobbler. "And the police have probably checked local pawnshops about the stolen merchandise already. A big zero."

"Maybe Spencer wasn't the robber after all." I dug into the bowl for a blackberry. "Audie said he came with good references. No one suspected him. I would have heard—you know how the grapevine works."

"Besides, he would have received one of those

threatening e-mails." Peppi spoke with assurance.

Dina and I stared at her.

"How did you know about that?" my sister demanded. Too late to warn her not to talk.

A satisfied look flew across Peppi's face. "I thought so." She grinned. "I stopped by Gaynor Goodies myself. The whole town has heard about the e-mails by now. I received one myself, just last night."

"You did!" Dina's nose quivered like our dog Ralphie's. "What is Elsie accusing you of?"

"Oh, she said I cheated on my essay and didn't deserve my internship at the paper."

Peppi spoke so carelessly that I couldn't believe any truth existed in the accusation.

"So what did Elsie accuse Spencer of?" Like any good reporter, Peppi refused to lose the scent trail.

I held my breath. I didn't want Dina spilling the beans about the second alias. I shouldn't have worried.

"Nothing specific." Dina sighed. "That's the problem. I know!" She dabbed at a blueberry on her face with a napkin.

"Maybe he had a partner. Someone who could help him fence stuff." Peppi offered her opinion.

"A partner." I mulled that over. That possibility had come up before. I tried to remember where I had first run across Spencer. "His name always comes up when people mention they need a cleaning service."

"Who uses—used—him?" Peppi asked.

"Good question!" Dina beamed at her friend as if she were her own personal discovery. In different circumstances I would laugh at the notion of my teen-aged sister mentoring Peppi, who looked like she was in her mid-twenties. She had appeared in Grace Gulch in the fall and thrown herself into community life, between school, the paper, and the theater. She also worked part-time as a waitress at The Gulch, the town's buffalo steak-and-potatoes restaurant.

Dina dug out the steno pad that she carried with her everywhere. "We know that he cleaned the theater. And I've seen him at the *Herald* offices. Cici, do you know what other businesses he cleaned for?"

I thought back to snippets of conversation from recent Chamber of Commerce meetings and gave her a few names. He cleaned half the businesses in our three-block downtown area, and it didn't seem to matter if the business was owned by a Grace or a Gaynor. If you needed a janitor, you used Spencer's services.

"But didn't he clean homes, too?" Peppi pointed out. "What about those customers? Do we know any of their names?"

We pondered that question while we each took another bite. "Audie may have a list of references," I said. "I'll ask him."

When we finished the cobbler, I paid for the check. What else did I expect, eating out with two college students? To give Dina credit, she left the tip.

"That's enough for one day. I need to get back to work," I told the girls when we buckled into my Civic. I checked my side view mirror and glanced over my shoulder. A van approached on the highway, but it didn't signal its intention to pull into the diner. I backed out of the parking space.

Crunch. I heard the sound of a taillight shattering, and the car rocked a little. The van I had expected to move down the road had instead turned into the parking lot—and the back of my car.

From: Elsie Holland (Snoozeulose@ggcc.com)
Date: Sunday, April 20, 9:39 PM
To: Cord Grace (cgrace.Circle_G@ggcoc.net)
Subject: Parking tickets?

Last month your truck failed the emissions test. You spoke with Officer Frances Waller and mysteriously received your renewal tag. Did you fix the problem. . .or the police?

Expect further communication from me on the subject.

Monday, April 21

I stopped the car and rid my mind of angry thoughts about irresponsible tourists.

Sure enough, the license tag indicated the driver came from out of state. Route 66 brought business to our county, but it also brought people who ignored traffic laws. The van driver had already pulled into an empty space, and a family with two small children, a rarity at a restaurant at midday, piled out. They appeared oblivious to the damage they had done to my car.

I sighed. My windshield suffered enough from the county's dirt roads; now I'd have to replace the taillights, too. *Oh, well.*

"What are you doing?" Dina's voice interrupted my thoughts.

Peppi had already unbuckled her seat belt and opened the door. She ran after the van driver, a young mother not much older than she, and screamed, "Hey! What's the matter with you? Why don't you look where you're going?"

The woman paused in mid-stride, holding on to her children's hands. "I'm sorry?"

"You ran into my friend's car." Peppi got a few inches away from the stranger's face.

Dina and I stared at Peppi, then at each other.

"Bounced us around in that car like ice cubes in a glass." Peppi didn't lower her voice. "What are you going to do about it?"

I'd heard enough. I got out of the car. "Peppi."

She didn't budge but instead pulled out her cell phone and started dialing.

I darted forward and grabbed the phone before she could finish dialing. "Peppi, please. I'll handle this." I turned to the startled family.

Two toddlers clung to their mother's skirt, their last defense against angry strangers.

I sought to soften their worry with a smile. "Excuse me, ma'am, I'm sure you didn't realize you dinged my car when you turned into the parking lot." I thought about apologizing for not looking, but I'd be lying, and I might open myself up for trouble. "We need to exchange insurance information."

"We—collided?"

Peppi sputtered.

"Look at my taillight." I spoke before Peppi could interrupt.

The mother studied the shattered plastic and appeared to take in the situation for the first time. Together, we looked at the front bumper of her van. Sure enough, we found a splinter of red glass that matched the center point of my broken taillight.

"I'm so sorry," she stammered.

Beside us, Dina coaxed Peppi back into the Civic. I exchanged insurance information with the woman. By the time I sat behind the steering wheel, Peppi's tirade had subsided to muttering under her breath.

We drove in silence for a few minutes while I waited for an apology from Peppi.

"Why did you let her get away with it?"

So much for an apology. "I have her insurance information." Although the more Peppi carried on, the less I wanted to pursue the matter.

"Careless drivers like that woman cause a lot of damage. Be sure you report her."

Why won't she let it go? "My car, my choice." I would think twice before inviting Peppi to accompany us again.

"Whoa, ladies," Dina piped up. "Don't worry, sis, Peppi overreacts to all kinds of things. Pop quizzes, last-minute changes at the paper—"

"But it's not right." Peppi spoke in self-defense, then shrugged. "Guilty as charged." She settled into the backseat and didn't speak of the accident again. An hour later we pulled into the parking lot behind the store.

"Anyone want some tea? Water?" That was me, always playing the perfect hostess. Although I wished Dina would take Peppi and disappear, I knew how thirsty we all were. The girls followed me into the storeroom. Dina fetched the bottled water while I listened to my messages.

Audie had called to remind me of the play rehearsal that night. The second call came from Frances Waller.

"Cici. I've got good news for you. Mrs. Mallory called up Chief Reiner, and he's agreed to let you go ahead and have the pearls back for the play as soon as we're done testing them. They should be ready on Thursday."

"That's great!" Dina had heard the message. As props person for the theater, she had goggled at the chance to use the Mallory pearls in the production.

"Some people think they can get anything they want." Peppi dipped her napkin in the water and wiped it across her forehead. "Only a Grace could get away with that. And only in Grace Gulch."

Here we go again. Peppi sounded ready to start another tirade, this time against the special privileges afforded to Magda Grace Mallory. Peppi's attitude didn't make sense. She sounded for all the world like a Gaynor holding a grudge against a Grace—a feud harking back to the founding of our town—although as far as I knew she had only recently moved to town and wasn't related to either clan.

The cold drink seemed to soothe her, and she let it go without further comment. "But I'm not complaining. I get to wear the pearls in the play."

"I don't care who pulled strings. I'm just glad we get to use the pearls. Only think." Dina's hazel eyes danced. "You should auction the pearls to the highest bidder. They'd bring a good price now that they're evidence in a murder investigation."

"The theater could use the funds." Even so, I would hold on to the pearls for a while. The police might change their minds and want them back.

In fact, that was what Frances implied. I had them back—for now. Oh, well. Eventually I could sell them to make a tidy profit for the store and the theatre.

"I know what I'll do." Dina pulled out her steno pad and made a note. "I'll write a piece for the paper, how the pearls that Peppi is wearing in the play are the same ones that were discovered with Spencer's body. That ought to sell a few more tickets. People will want front row seats, just to ogle them."

Peppi laughed at that, and the earlier uneasiness I felt about her dissipated.

"Are we going to check out more pawnshops tomorrow?" Dina asked.

Peppi shook her head. "I've got classes and work, and then there's my aerobics class at the gym. I can't make it."

"You work out all the time. You can afford to miss one class." Dina chided her friend. "But you're right. Work and school for me, too." Her hazel eyes warned me not to go sleuthing on my own.

The girls left a few minutes later, and I debated about what to do until the rehearsal started. Since they wouldn't wear costumes until the last few rehearsals, I didn't need to attend these early run-throughs. But I enjoyed watching Audie at work. He had a knack for getting the most out of his amateur actors, even people like Reiner, who portrayed a police officer in the play. Audie had teased me about coming to the theater every night. I smiled when I remembered the conversation.

"Watch out. If you come here any more often, you'll catch the acting bug." Audie's eyes had swept over me as if assessing me for a role.

I blushed under his appraisal. "The only thing I want

to catch at the theater is the director."

In answer, he kissed me.

Before tonight's rehearsal I went home long enough to mix together a cold pasta salad for a late supper, and then I headed over to the MGM.

The same soupcon of pleasure the theater always gave me tingled my fingers when I walked into the dark back of the auditorium. Even in the dim light coming from the stage, the room reminded me of the Paris Opera House in *Phantom of the Opera*, the inspiration behind the design.

As expected, most of the cast had already assembled. I timed my arrival to avoid a barrage of questions from them. They would get their chance soon enough at the first break.

The players sounded like a Who's Who of Grace Gulch, heavily weighted in favor of the Grace family. In addition to Magda, other Graces included Mayor Ron, as Uncle Teddy; my friend Cord, as Jonathan; and Magda's son, Gene Mallory, playing the sinister Dr. Gilchrist. Gene's Shih Tzu dog, Bobo, accompanied him to every rehearsal; Audie joked about listing him with the cast members. Theater regular Suzanne Jay would play the second Brewster sister; she and Magda shared a passing resemblance that made the connection believable. The plum role of Mortimer Brewster had fallen to Lauren Packer. In spite of his vulture-sharp nose and thin lips, he oozed charm on stage.

Like Chief Reiner, Frances Waller had been roped into playing a police officer in the play. When not on duty, she showed at most rehearsals, chatting with various cast members, especially Cord.

Peppi rounded out the cast, the only unknown,

but she won the part fair and square with her excellent acting ability. The group made her feel welcome to the community.

The one person missing from tonight's rehearsal was Magda herself.

Audie stood in the orchestra pit. My poor fiancé attempted to give instructions to the actors, but everyone kept asking him about the discovery of the body. I took pity on him and joined him in front of the stage. "Maybe we should just tell them and get it over with," I whispered in his ear.

He shrugged, a familiar twinkle dancing in his eyes, then addressed the group. "Yes, I discovered Victor Spencer's body on Saturday night. Yes, it was the same man who cleaned the theater. Yes, it was murder. Yes, he had Magda's pearls. No, we don't know why he was at Cici's store. And that's really all we know."

A chorus of questions erupted on stage, but Audie raised his hand. "And that's all I'm going to say on the matter for now. Back to work." He brushed my cheek with his lips, and I headed for the back to prepare drinks for the rehearsal break.

Magda arrived. "Sorry I'm late!" she said in greeting to the assembled cast. She spoke to Audie in a whisper that reached me where I hovered in the wings.

"I've been with the police. I confirmed your whereabouts for last night."

So that's where Audie was last night. With Magda. Relief washed over me. Reiner could stop suspecting Audie in Spencer's death. I came forward and hugged Magda.

"Thanks!"

Magda stepped back, surprise written on her face. She

and Audie looked as guilty as a pair of kids with a broken cookie jar. She shrugged in an elaborate "I-didn't-know-she-was-there" apology to Audie. A grimace crossed his face.

I didn't get it. So what if Audie met with Magda last night? After all, she owned the theater and technically was his employer.

Audie didn't give me time to think about it. He pecked me on my cheek. "I told you not to worry," he whispered in my ear. Out loud, he called, "Attention on stage!"

With Magda's arrival, rehearsal could begin. I would have to wait for my answers yet again.

As soon as the actors started rehearsing their lines, I busied myself preparing cold beverages for the break. Whatever the time of year, stage lights kept the stage warm, and it didn't take long to work up a thirst. So I fixed pitchers of iced tea and water.

The next hour sped by while the cast blocked out the scenes from the first act. The first pitcher of tea disappeared fast; cast members grabbed a glass while they waited for their next cue. I watched the action on stage in between refilling drinks. It was amazing how much attention to detail went into giving a play the illusion of reality. Come opening night, the audience would believe that the set really was the living room of the Brewster home. Dina made notes of all the changes in her ever-present steno notebook.

When Audie called a break, Mayor Ron arrived at the tea table first. He gulped down a glass of water in a single, long swallow. "Feels good to wet the whistle. Thanks." Ever the politician, he made a point to thank everyone for the smallest favor. I liked the man more than ever for throwing himself into the role of zany Uncle Teddy, an over-the-top performance that would leave the audience in stitches. I toyed with the idea of giving him a toupee to cover his bald head and a handlebar mustache to echo the connection to Theodore Roosevelt and the charge up San Juan Hill. It was hard to believe we had suspected him in Penn Hardy's death only a few months ago.

Everyone except the mayor plopped in velvet-cushioned seats after grabbing their drinks. He stood in front and raised his voice—one that didn't need the help of a microphone to be heard.

"My office will be making an important announcement tomorrow morning at nine, in front of the city office building. I hope you can all be there."

8

From: Elsie Holland (Snoozeulose@ggcc.com)
Date: Monday, April 21, 9:35 PM
To: Ronald Grace (rgrace@gg.gov)
Subject: Campaign Funding

You reported only $1,000 spent on last year's reelection campaign. Your newspaper advertising alone cost at least that much. What are you trying to hide?

Expect further communication from me on the subject.

Tuesday, April 22

Mayor Ron must have sensed the disinterest in the upcoming press conference. No one wanted to get up early—well, early after staying up late for rehearsal—to hear about plans for the Memorial Day parade or something equally distant.

He winked. "It concerns the theater."

That caught our attention. He refused to give any further details. Since I worked in town, I decided to check it out. Dina, and maybe Peppi, would be there, of course, to cover breaking news for the *Herald*. I wondered who else would show up besides Magda, as owner, and Audie, as director.

The next morning, I locked the door to my store to attend the press conference. The entire cast had assembled to hear the announcement, as well as the city council and a handful of other citizens, including the community college art teacher. Dina and Peppi waited by the podium where the mayor would make his announcement. Cord arrived in his truck, along with his temporary ranch hand and cousin, Gene Mallory, and his ever present companion, Bobo the dog. Frances left the city building, which also housed police headquarters and walked across the street to join them. I caught sight of Lauren leaving his office.

Since my store was closed until repairs were finished, I had dressed in contemporary clothing. It felt good to wear jeans and a T-shirt, like everyone else, and not be stifled in a bustle. I still pulled my rowdy hair back in a bun to keep it as neat as possible.

At one minute past nine, the mayor walked through the glass doors of the city building, accompanied by his sister Magda Mallory. Audie trailed the two.

Mayor Ron studied the assembled group. If the sparse audience disappointed him, he didn't let it show. He beamed at us and stepped onto the platform, tapping the microphone to make sure it was live.

He began in his usual fashion, with the grand and glorious history of Grace Gulch. And if he emphasized the role of the Grace family in the growth of the town, who could blame him? After all, the town was named after his ancestor, Bob Grace, who claimed the first parcel of land in the land run of 1891. Today the mayor told the story of how Bob's wife, Mary, founded a theater where the MGM stood today and brought culture to the frontier.

That was true. I took pride in those pioneer women,

my own great-grandmother among them. They brought beauty, music, theater, and literature with them, determined not to leave civilization behind. Thanks to them, Grace Gulch boasted a great library for a town our size, a well-designed, year-round theater, and a good music education system for both children and adults. Unfortunately, the visual arts lagged behind. The occasional exhibits at the community college fell far below the standard set by the Philbrook and Gilcrease museums in Tulsa.

"It is our responsibility to continue that fine tradition. And to that end, we plan to open an up-to-date Center for the Arts right here in Grace Gulch." He beckoned for Magda to come closer. "It is my pleasure to introduce my sister, Magda Grace Mallory."

Magda, gray hair perfectly coiffed in spite of the stiff breeze blowing across the square, took her place behind the mike.

"It has always been my dream to bring Mary Grace's dreams to fruition and to put Grace Gulch on the twenty-first-century map of Oklahoma culture. The theater was the first step in that dream. By this time next year, we will begin construction on a museum that will feature the best local, western, and national artists."

The mayor handed her a spool of fabric, and together they unwound the length. The banner read GRACE GULCH CENTER FOR THE ARTS. I could imagine it going into the mayor's office along with his other Grace memorabilia.

The audience responded with polite applause. Some kind of sports venue—say a new ball field—would have inspired more enthusiasm. But of course Magda Mallory, Grace Gulch's leading patron of the arts, would suggest a museum.

My thoughts wandered. An art museum—that might draw my errant older sister back home. Jenna lived in Taos, New Mexico, and made her living buying and selling the fine artwork available there. Jenna, back in Grace Gulch? The idea left me unsettled.

A more urgent thought intruded. The museum—that must have been the subject of the secret meeting between Audie and Magda on the night of the murder. Maybe she asked him to keep it a secret until after the public announcement.

"At this time, the city council—" here she gestured at the group assembled behind her—"is holding a contest for the design of the museum and will seek construction bids by the beginning of summer."

Audie approached the mike next. He looked handsome in his cream colored linen suit with the light breeze blowing his Nordic blond hair into casual disarray.

"'We live in an age when unnecessary things are our only necessities.' Oscar Wilde said that over a hundred years ago, but it's still true today. We are fortunate to live in a country where we don't often have to worry about physical needs like food, shelter, and clothing. We are free to indulge in spiritual necessities such as beauty, art, and culture." He made a few congratulatory remarks about the Center for the Arts—how it would put Grace Gulch on the national cultural map and bring more tourists to our town and improve the quality of life and all that—and ended with a plug for the upcoming production of *Arsenic and Old Lace*. He thanked Magda for her support of the theater and stepped away from the mike.

After the mayor ended his presentation, Dina peppered him with questions like a veteran. Peppi had questions for Audie and Magda, as well, so I decided to talk with my fiancé later.

"Want some coffee?" Frances Waller tapped me on my elbow. Out of uniform and with a touch of makeup, she looked lovely.

"Sure." My stomach rumbled, reminding me that I had skipped breakfast.

We walked in the direction of Gaynor Goodies. Cord lingered by the door to the bakery, face twisted in a frown. I followed the direction of his gaze—Gene Mallory. Magda's son slipped into the crowd, hurrying away to some unknown destination, his dog, Bobo, trotting along behind.

Then Cord caught sight of us, and he smiled. Frances's step beside me quickened, a light color in her cheeks.

"Good morning. I was hoping you'd join me." Cord's voice rumbled with something more than friendship as we walked through the door.

We paid for our purchases and found a table by the front window.

"I hope you don't mind." Cord arched an eyebrow at me. "I want to keep an eye out for Gene. Since we arrived together, I guess I have to wait for him to come back before I can leave." He dunked a cake doughnut in black coffee. "Want some?" He offered a taste to Frances. She took a bite and giggled, sounding for the moment like she was back in high school.

I felt like a fifth wheel and wondered where Audie was. The doorbell jingled, and he walked in and waved at us. He bought a cup of Chai tea and a bagel and joined us at the table.

I wanted to ask Audie if Magda's announcement was

his big secret, but I wouldn't, not in front of Cord and Frances. Instead, I pursued the topic of Gene Mallory with Cord.

"How is your cousin working out?"

I could guess the answer from the change in his demeanor. *Not well.* Look at the way Gene had left Cord without a word after the press conference. Everyone knew that Magda had pressured Cord into taking on his cousin as a ranch hand.

"I wish I'd never agreed to let Gene work at the ranch." The black expression on Cord's face rivaled his coffee. "His work is slipshod. Old Bob Grace might have been a cowhand, but I seem to be the only Grace left alive who likes ranch work."

"Maybe it's Mrs. Mallory's version of tough love." Frances had edged her chair a few inches closer to Cord while they shared the dunking doughnut. "Spend a few months on the ranch and learn what it means to work for your living."

"Something like that." Cord frowned. "Of course, Gene hung around the ranch when I was growing up. He helped out for a couple of summers, but he didn't like it any more than Uncle Ron or Aunt Magda did. He never wanted to come back after he went to college. But that degree hasn't done him much good. He seems content to live off family money." He laughed, more like a cough. "That little dog of his might make a decent sheepherder, but Gene doesn't fit in."

Family money. The reason for Gene's upset departure clicked. "So every time Magda takes on one of these projects—"

"He sees his inheritance dwindling," Cord agreed gloomily.

"At least he doesn't blame me or the theater," Audie said. "Maybe all that angst is what makes him so good at playing Dr. Gilchrist in the play."

Cord grunted. "Maybe you can make an actor out of him." He grinned. "Hey, if you can turn me into Jonathan Brewster—" At the mention of the sinister Brewster cousin, Cord twisted his face and looked as ugly as Raymond Massey in the movie—"Maybe you can make something out of Gene. I sure haven't succeeded at the ranch. Aunt Magda thinks he'll turn around fine once he finds his purpose in life, but if he hasn't figured that out at his age. . . ."

I thought about Jenna, who was close in age to the Mallory heir. Two restless souls.

"With God, all things are possible." Audie crunched on his bagel. "He led me here, and it was hardly what I expected when I finished college."

"Well maybe God will lead Gene to take your place in Chicago." Cord smirked.

Before I could protest, Cord lifted his hands in a gesture of self-defense.

"Just kidding. You're right, Audie. I should pray for him instead of complaining. I do. It's only that I hate having to do his work and paying him for it on top of that." Cord found a last bite of doughnut on his napkin and offered it to Frances.

She shook her head. "I need to be on my way. I'm supposed to report to work before long."

Jessie approached with a coffee carafe. Today she wore a uniform in robin's egg blue with embroidered birds on her apron. I thought about the message Spencer was holding and remembered the e-mail Jessie had received.

"Hey, Jessie, have you heard anything more from that Elsie Holland person?"

She blinked her brown eyes, twice. "Why, no. I figure it was just a practical joke."

"Elsie Holland?" Cord spoke up. "Has she been writing to you, too?"

"I take it you've received one of her threats, then?" Audie sipped the fresh coffee. "Welcome to the club."

"She's also written to Dina and Peppi that we know of," I explained. I didn't mention the e-mail sent to Spencer.

Cord whistled through his teeth. "And me. And Frances. I take it they're all about the same? Some foolish rumor and threatening to contact us about it?"

We nodded our heads in agreement.

Cord's color heightened, but I didn't ask him for details. "Do you know who she is?"

We explained our theory about Elsie Holland being an alias.

"Whoever 'Elsie' may be, he or she is playing with fire." Audie frowned. "Sooner or later, she'll hit too close to the truth, and someone may decide to retaliate."

"She wouldn't have to dig too far for dirt on my cousin. Speaking of which, there he is, the old lazybones."

We all looked out the window at the subject of our discussion. Tall, with brown hair streaked with blond thanks to the hours spent in the sun at the ranch, Gene could be considered handsome except for the scowl that marred his face. Bobo trotted along behind him. My heart softened. No man who inspired a dog's undying affection could be all bad.

"Well I'd best be going before he decides to disappear again," Cord said.

My thoughts turned to my own family situation. At least no one had ever asked me to try to rein in my irresponsible older sister. I filled that role with Dina.

"Will I see you at rehearsal tonight?" Audie gathered the empty cups for the trash.

"If you promise to eat supper with me after. I've made up a batch of Frito chili pie."

"Then plan on it." Audie whistled while he walked me back to the store.

Once again I wondered what difference the new arts complex would make. Would this mean a new opportunity for him, as director of the whole shebang? I hoped so. I waited for him to tell me that Magda's announcement was his secret. But he left me at my front door and continued on his way without saying a word about it.

Tonight, I told myself. *He'll tell me tonight.*

The day sped by as I made arrangements for repairs to the store. After some debate, I decided to do some minor remodeling and advertise for a "Grand Reopening" in the Sunday edition of the *Grace Gulch Herald*. This afternoon the glazier would replace my front window. After I called the carpenter to come tomorrow, I spent time researching the computer for decorating ideas. Along with the new floor, I wanted new paint, curtains, rugs—the works. *Too bad Jenna isn't here.* My sister had an excellent eye for design; I guessed it went with her ability as an art dealer.

As promised I hurried to the theater after I left the store. One by one, cast members congratulated Magda on the Center for the Arts. Her announcement had replaced Spencer's murder as the topic of prerehearsal buzz.

"What a grand idea!" That came from Peppi.

"When do you expect to open?" Dina asked a reporter's

questions. "Is there a chance we'll get to see your private collection?" Magda had mentioned she would leave her own pieces of art to the new museum.

All the cast members seemed happy about the news, that is, except for the one conspicuous absence—Gene. Audie called the rehearsal to order, and Magda and Suzanne Jay as the Brewster sisters had decided to end the lonely life of their latest guest.

From my vantage point at the drinks table, I saw the door open wide and Gene march down the center aisle to the orchestra pit. Bobo ran beside him, letting out small yips. A few heads in the auditorium turned, but the people on stage didn't notice.

"The gentleman died because he drank some wine with poison in it. Now I don't know why you're making such a big deal over this, Mortimer. Don't you worry about a thing!" Magda, as Abby Brewster, explained the reason for a dead body in the window seat to her nephew.

"Mother!" Gene bellowed in his bass voice.

Audie, too intent on the action on stage to notice Gene's approach, whirled around. "Excuse me? Gene? We're in mid-rehearsal."

Gene jumped up on stage and confronted Magda.

"This is too much. I know you love this theater. And then your plans for the Center for the Arts. That was bad enough. But why did you put all that money in a trust fund? Do you think it's your responsibility to keep it running even after you're dead?"

9

From: Elsie Holland (Snoozeulose@ggcc.com)
Date: Monday, April 21, 9:41 PM
To: Eugene Mallory (GMallory.Circle_G@ggcoc.net)
Subject: Tough love?

Magda Grace Mallory recently made you return to work at the Circle G Ranch. Public opinion implies she wants to toughen you up.

My question is this: What did you do that made your mother so upset? I believe I know.

Expect further communication from me on the subject.

Tuesday, April 22

No one knew how to respond to Gene's harsh words. Magda's face, already pale in the glare of the stage lights, blanched. "That's private business, Gene. We'll discuss it at home."

Audie moved between them. "Gene, you're upset. Why don't you go on home?"

Fury transformed Gene's face to the point that he resembled his character in the play. The sinister Dr. Gilchrist performed multiple facial reconstructions on Jonathan Brewster until he resembled Frankenstein. But Gene took a deep breath and unclenched his fists, dropping his hands to his sides.

Gene pointed a finger at Audie's chest and then at the audience. "You're stealing my inheritance, every one of you. You all have a reason to keep the theater running. Unless Mother changes her mind, you can look for someone else to play the dear old doctor. I know when I'm not wanted."

In the silence following his remarks, he stormed down the aisle and out the door.

"I'm sorry, Audie dear." Magda had regained some of her composure. "I'd better go speak with him, don't you think?" She departed the stage.

Lauren Packer murmured an apology and followed her. As Magda's lawyer, he must want to discuss the situation with the family. He would have written the trust agreement, after all.

The departure of three actors tore a hole in Audie's plans for the night. He looked lost. Had he known about Magda's provision for the theater or had the news surprised him?

Audie clapped his hands and whistled for everyone's attention. The low murmur of conversation ceased.

"In view of the, um, unexpected developments, we'll call it a night." His eyes twinkled. "Just come back tomorrow night prepared to work twice as hard."

After Audie's announcement, the theater emptied in a few minutes. I put the tea and ice water in the refrigerator, ready for the next rehearsal.

Only Dina lingered. I could guess what she wanted to talk about—Gene's outburst and its implications. A scoop all her own. She wouldn't dare put speculation or the vague hints that Gene had dropped in the *Herald*. But if she could confirm the information. . .

And if Dina didn't jump the gun, Peppi might. She had left with the rest of the cast. Was she heading for the newspaper office even now to write up the events of the night?

No, I decided. As an intern Peppi didn't have that kind of power. Her reporting consisted primarily of covering the police blotter.

Dina tagged along behind Audie as he made his rounds, locking up the theater for the night. I couldn't hear their conversation, but she gestured to the stage, and he shook his head in refusal. By the time they reached me, her face had turned almost as pink as her hair.

Tone it down or you'll never become a successful reporter. A good reporter had to be persistent, but belligerence would drive people away.

"C'mon, give me something. You know the grapevine will have the news about the scene here tonight all over town by morning. And my editor will expect me to know what went down since I'm Miss Johnny-on-the-spot."

"Not yet. And that's final." Audie smiled to soften his refusal. "I don't know anything for certain, and I need to discuss it with Magda before I tell the world. I promise that as soon as I know something solid, you will be the first to hear about it." He nodded in my direction. "After my fiancée, of course."

Dina scowled but accepted Audie's limits. "I'll expect details tomorrow night. Or sooner." Her face had returned to its normal color, and she grinned, her good spirits restored. She bid us good night and walked out, leaving us finally, blissfully, alone.

"I thought she'd never leave." Audie blew the air out of his cheeks and put his arms around me.

I leaned into his chest, welcoming the warmth and security. We stayed that way for a long moment, not speaking until Audie pulled away.

"I intend to go see Magda and find out what this is all about. Do you want to come with me?"

"I thought you'd never ask."

We each drove our own cars to Magda's house, a two-story brick-and-stone edifice that Bob Grace had built for Mary in town when his ranch prospered. The porch light turned on as soon as I pulled my Civic into the drive, as if Magda had anticipated company.

By the time Audie parked on the street, Magda had come outside to greet us. The normally lovely matron looked haggard, a great weight wearing her down. "Audie, Cici. I'm so glad you stopped by. Please come in."

We followed her into her formal parlor and sat on chairs that Mary Grace had decorated with needlepoint. Soft light glowed from genuine Tiffany lamps. "Would you like something to drink?"

Audie shook his head. My mouth felt as parched as a baseball diamond in mid-July. "I'll have a glass of water, if it's not too much trouble."

Minutes passed before Magda returned. She set out tall goblets on china coasters and poured water from a cut-glass pitcher.

Hostess duties dispensed, Magda plunged into business. "I'm so sorry that Gene disrupted the rehearsal the way that he did. I meant to tell you the news, privately, of course."

"What was he talking about?" Audie didn't dance around the question.

"I have set up a trust fund to finance the Center for the Arts, including the theater, of course. Gene does not share my passion for the arts; and I want to provide for its future after my passing. I told him tonight."

No wonder Gene was upset. From his vantage point, the theater was stealing his birthright. How would I feel if Dad mortgaged the family ranch and gave the money away?

"That's very generous of you." Audie managed a gracious response.

Magda must have sensed my doubts. "You needn't worry about Gene. I have also set up a trust fund for him."

If Cord was right about Gene, a trust fund would protect his cousin from squandering a lump sum inheritance. But Magda would never admit that to us.

"I was so pleased when the two of you became engaged." Magda refilled our glasses. "That stirred me into action. Audie, you should know you have a job here in Grace Gulch as long as you wish to stay."

What a grand wedding present!

Audie flushed and stammered a thank-you. Why did he look uneasy? I was ecstatic, myself.

Magda turned her violet eyes in my direction. "Saturday evening, Audie and I were discussing the terms of his contract. When I went to Lauren's office to set up the trust funds, I also asked him to draw up the paperwork." She smiled, a benevolent dictator who had arranged things to her satisfaction. "There is no hurry, but I would like to settle the matter as my wedding gift to you."

"I explained that I needed time to consider her generous offer," Audie told me.

Why did he want to wait? The same hesitant undercurrents I had sensed all week returned, tugging at my spirit. But I refused to worry about it. Instead I returned to the subject of the morning's press conference.

"The new arts center sounds wonderful. How are those plans coming?"

Magda waved her hands. "We want to do it right. Architectural designs are due by the first of May, and we will make our decision a month after that. Of course, that is only the start." She settled back in her chair, her water glass held by her slender fingers. "Now tell me. Have the police returned the pearls to you yet?"

"No. They promise it will be soon."

"Good." She smiled, revealing even teeth well preserved for someone of her age. "I want you to wear them, Cici. Don't keep them hidden away in the box until the play. Pearls lose their luster if you don't wear them, you know."

The old maxim wasn't exactly true. In fact, skin oils could harm the jewels; pearls worn frequently required extra care. I suspected Magda knew that but she wanted me to enjoy them before I sold them, all the same.

"I'll do that," I promised.

"It's been a long day." She stood. "If you will excuse me?"

We took our cue and departed. A flurry of questions for Audie rushed through my head. Did he intend to sign the new contract? Was there a problem with it? Knowing Magda, I believed it must be fair. Another thought struck me. Was he holding out for something else—like a position as the director of the entire arts complex and not only the theater? I decided to invite him home so we could talk.

Audie followed me out onto the driveway.

"Care to come over for a cup of coffee?" I asked.

Audie shook his head. "Not tonight. Magda's right. It's been a long day." He kissed me on the cheek and walked to his car.

I wouldn't learn the answers today. But Magda's promise of a lifetime contract for Audie buoyed my spirits. Once in bed, I drifted to sleep, visions of my fiancé as director of the arts complex dancing through my dreams. He had never mentioned any interest in working outside the theater world, and no one more qualified to run the complex existed in all of Grace Gulch. Lincoln County, for that matter. I couldn't believe the trust fund Magda had set up. Security was a luxury that most people in the theatrical world did not enjoy.

My dreams had Audie retiring from a long and illustrious career that won Grace Gulch international respect in the arts world. When I woke up, I came back down to earth. There were other candidates for the position. The high school music teacher, who also worked with the community chorus, might want to apply for the job, or the arts professor at the community college. They could even bring in someone from the outside. After all, Magda had hired Audie away from Chicago.

On Wednesday morning, still in a hopeful mood, I dressed in one of my favorite vintage outfits, a dreamy gauze skirt and blouse from the sixties. I called it my gypsy outfit. What should I do after I let the carpenter in to work on the floor? Take care of online business, like a responsible store owner, or hunt down Spencer's killer?

I should concentrate on my business. This was the perfect time to develop an idea I had toyed with. Customers could insert a photo of their face onto a particular style and see if they liked it or not before they placed an order. But while the concept seemed simple, I didn't know how to program it into the computer, so it stayed filed in the "maybe someday" file in my brain.

Let me be honest. I *wanted* to track down the murderer. The best lead lay in finding the blackmailer. For that I would need Dina's help at the college. I would call her from the store. But first I decided to stop at gossip central, Gaynor Goodies.

My hippie outfit put me in the mood for some health food, so I opted for multigrain muffins. Of course all the customers wanted to talk with me. They either wanted to discuss the murder or the uproar at the theater last night, or both. I couldn't believe that four days after Spencer's murder, I knew almost nothing more than I did on the night Audie discovered his body in the store. By this time after the gunfight last fall, we had identified the primary suspects. Beyond our surmise that Spencer was a burglar and had a partner, we had made no progress at all. Zilch.

Gaynor Goodies thrived on the local grapevine. Maybe I could find the grains of truth behind the blackmail rumors. So I answered questions as simply as possible and then I listened. People liked hearing themselves talk.

They threw out a dozen names of possible murder suspects. Every store owner made the list, with Gaynors pointing fingers at Graces and vice versa. The general theory was that Vic Spencer had uncovered some skulduggery at one of the businesses and was killed to silence him.

But in that case, Spencer was the blackmailer, and not the one being blackmailed. The police asked me to keep quiet about the blackmail note in Spencer's possession.

That seemed like the most promising angle to me. I wondered if I could get into his office and see if he had left any hints there about blackmail. Probably not. Besides, that was illegal entry.

A few people commented on Vic's connection with the theater and the exciting news about Center for the Arts, and did I think Audie would get to manage the whole shebang or would he stay with the theater only? I gave them noncommittal answers and didn't mention the negotiations—the exact nature of which I still did not know—between Audie and Magda.

One name kept popping up: Lauren Packer. That made sense, given his position as Magda's lawyer, the creator of the trust funds, and one of Spencer's many clients downtown. On top of that, he was involved with the theater. More than one person suggested him as possible director for the arts complex.

I thought of the way Lauren had run after Magda after Gene's outburst last night. Did he want to work his way further into her plans for the complex? Did he resent Audie's friendship with Magda? I felt a moment's trepidation. Audie made a great theater director, but how would he manage against a wily courtroom attorney?

Then I remembered Magda's reassurances last night. She knew what she wanted, and she could outmaneuver anybody. Still, common sense suggested a discussion about the lawyer with Audie at some point.

The better part of an hour passed before I left, with a few more rumors and theories and nothing more by way of solid facts.

"Come back any time!" Jessie winked at me. "You're good for business." She leaned forward and handed me a cup of mocha latté. "On the house. Just let me know when you figure out what's happening with Frances."

Frances? What was that all about? I waved good-bye and opened my store a few minutes before the carpenter would arrive. The phone rang as soon as I stepped inside. I grabbed the handset. "Hello?"

"I need to reschedule our lunch date."

From: Jerry Burton (cbtrotter@redbud.net)
Date: Tuesday, April 22, 9:34 PM
To: Suzanne Jay (SJay_MGM@ggcoc.net)
Subject: Coincidence?

A recent edition of the Grace Gulch Herald
reported that you will be playing the part of
Martha Brewster in the upcoming production of
Arsenic and Old Lace *at the MGM Theater. You*
bear a striking resemblance to the actress playing
the role of Abby Brewster, Magda Grace Mallory
herself. Coincidence?

Expect further communication from me on the
subject.

Wednesday, April 23

Suzanne Jay's voice stirred up guilt. I had totally forgotten our usual Wednesday lunch date. The leading
lady of the theater had come to know the Lord in the
course of the investigation into Penn Hardy's death last
fall. As his former mistress, she was one of the leading
suspects. Since her decision to follow Christ, we met once
a week for Bible study and discipleship time. Our growing
friendship pleased Audie, who always had a soft spot for
the actress.

Wednesdays at noon, Suzanne stopped by the store, and I'd put the CLOSED sign on the door for an hour, sometimes an hour and a half. She rarely missed.

"Magda has asked me to lunch with her. I'm sure you understand."

I did. Magda ruled Grace Gulch with a generous but firm hand. Most of the time we gladly acquiesced to her benevolent dictatorship. Coming at this point, however, I wondered if the invitation had anything to do with last night's revelations. But what could Gene's rant have to do with Suzanne?

"Oh?" I left the question open-ended, hoping my friend might tell me more.

"She called me this morning." Suzanne didn't rise to the bait.

"No problem. We'll meet tomorrow instead."

"Can't do it tomorrow, either. We're supposed to go to the nursing home with Enid Waldberg, remember?"

I stifled a groan. Why had I given in to Enid's pleas in a moment of weakness? I heard a page rustling over the phone wire, as if Suzanne were consulting a calendar.

"Will Friday work?"

"Of course." Something about Suzanne's tone of voice indicated today's meeting with Magda was anything but a casual luncheon, but she seemed reluctant to reveal more. Maybe an indirect question would prime the pump. "Speaking of Magda, though, what did you think of the bombshell Gene dropped last night? About a trust fund for the theater?"

"I think it's wonderful, although I'm sorry Gene is so upset." Her voice colored warmly, losing all of its earlier hesitation. "I'd hate to see anything happen to the theater.

Perhaps that's selfish of me." She let out an apologetic giggle.

"Nonsense. You're a great actress who needs a stage to share your talent."

I had scarcely hung up the receiver before the phone rang again. It was Dina.

"Can we come over? Peppi and me?"

Out my newly restored window, I saw the carpenter pull up in his truck. "Not right now. Smithy just got here to fix the floor."

"We'll be there at lunchtime, then. I'll bring the food this time." She clicked off her cell phone before I could respond.

True to her word, Dina arrived with Peppi, carrying fragrant bags from The Gulch. I wondered what mischief my sister had up her sleeve. She usually only bothered with The Gulch when she needed serious help.

"Okay, what trouble did you get into this time?"

"Let's eat first." Today Dina wore a lilac-colored T-shirt that coordinated with her pink hair.

We dug into the food, but Peppi couldn't keep quiet for long.

"We have a plan for catching the blackmailer."

"Don't be so modest." Dina flashed a grin at both of us. "She figured it out."

"Well, every e-mail we've seen has been written after 9:30 at night. I work at the library at the college, and so I checked a few things. 'Elsie Holland' has been using one of the library computers every night between 9:30 and 10:00."

I gulped down the bite of my sandwich. "What? Do you know who it is?"

Peppi shook her head. "You can't see the computers from the circulation desk where I sit."

"But we came up with a plan." Now Dina jumped in. "I'm going to show up tonight, pretending to have plans after work with Peppi. And I'll wander around and see if I can find this Elsie person."

"You're not going alone."

Two heads—one pink and one carrot red—turned in my direction.

"That's what I thought you'd say." Dina grinned at me.

We talked strategy and agreed to get together after prayer meeting to go to the library.

But first I had to get through the early evening. A minute past five, my front door rattled where Audie waited, his nose pressed to the glass.

"Ready?" He grinned like he had just received word that he had been nominated for a Tony award. He picked me up and twirled me around, my gypsy gauze skirt flying in a wild circle. The dreamy feel of the night before returned. Forget about murders and trust funds and blackmail.

Tonight before prayer meeting we would meet with Pastor Waldberg for mandatory premarital counseling. Maybe we would resolve more details for the wedding. We had reserved the date, the second Saturday in June, months ago, but we had decided very little else.

"Put me down." I made a halfhearted protest. "People will see you."

"I don't care!" Audie sang out. "I love Cici Wilde, and I want the world to know it!" After one more twirl, he set me back on my feet, kissing me before he let me go. "We need to leave if we're going to make it to our appointment on time."

I thought about walking. In my present mood the five blocks would float by under my feet. But no, by the time prayer meeting ended I would need my car to drive to the library. I made do with walking to the car hand in hand with Audie. I struggled to lock the back door with my left hand.

"Here. Let me help." Audie added his free hand.

Giggling, we managed to get it secured between us. How I looked forward to a lifetime of doing everything together, hand in hand. On the flip side, I wouldn't mind skipping the meeting with the pastor. How would his hellfire-and-brimstone style preaching translate into premarital counseling? Would he make dire warnings about lifetime commitment and marital vows? *Stop worrying,* I scolded myself. *He's a man of God who loves his people.*

Audie opened the passenger door for me. "'He who finds a wife finds what is good and receives favor from the Lord.'"

"Now I know that isn't Oscar Wilde."

"No." Audie grinned. "Solomon. Proverbs 18:22. I thank God every day for His favor in finding you." He lifted my hand to his lips and kissed it.

How I love this man.

"We'll be fine." He drove to the church parking lot nearest the office doors.

Pastor Waldberg met us at the door. Warmth shone in his dark eyes, his thick black brows raised in welcome. "Thank you for coming early." He led us back to his study.

After sitting on an uncomfortable-looking wooden chair, he tipped forward and looked straight at us, seriousness settling on his features. "I'm sure the two of you have given considerable thought to the marriage covenant. God plans for marriage to be a permanent commitment between two people. A picture of the unity between Christ and His bride, the church."

Audie reached out for my hand and squeezed my fingers. "I know that Cici is the woman God has planned for me." He spoke with absolute assurance.

I melted inside. I had dreamed about this kind of love my whole life. "And I feel the same way about Audie." I squeezed his fingers back, a bit of a kiss by way of fingertips and pulses.

"It is always a pleasure to see two committed Christians come before me." The pastor's face relaxed a tad, and he actually smiled. He read from Ephesians 5 and reminded us of the roles of a husband and wife. I knew Paul admonished wives to submit to their husbands, although I was enough of a twenty-first-century American woman to squirm a bit at the implications. Somehow my responsibility paled, though, in light of the apostle's exhortation for husbands to lay their lives on the line for their wives, as Christ loved the church.

Next the pastor pulled papers from his desk. "Here is a compatibility assessment I recommend that all couples take. It may indicate how well suited you are for marriage to each other—although of course it is not the final answer. God does not always lead by way of scientific method. I will give it to you to take home and complete it before our next session."

Compatibility?

When we were together, I felt like the other half of Audie, yin to his yang, but what secrets would a test uncover? His background as an only child growing up in a Chicago suburb was so different from mine, the middle child on a ranch. But I reminded myself, Audie had sought out our ranching community. No need to worry.

"Have you reached a decision about your ceremony?" Pastor Waldberg asked.

I must have looked confused. I thought the ceremony was a package deal—dating back hundreds of years to the first edition of the Book of Common Prayer and adapted over the centuries. With a sermon tacked on by the pastor, of course, in case unsaved heathens showed up at the ceremony, and warning us of the pitfalls we faced.

"I thought we might write our own vows." Audie smiled at me. "Remember, I mentioned that to you when we were looking at invitations? I promise I won't plagiarize any lines from a play. Not even Oscar Wilde." He pulled a small notebook, like the one he used for rehearsal notes, from his shirt pocket. "I've started on mine, but I'm not ready to share them yet."

That's right, he had. I had totally forgotten his suggestion. I couldn't even decide what dresses I wanted for the wedding party. Dina was the writer in the family. A nervous giggle bubbled through my lips.

One glance at Audie told me he was serious. Audie the artist, Audie the actor, Audie who could quote endless lines from both the Bible and Oscar Wilde, would not feel threatened by the idea of jotting down and remembering a few heartfelt lines. Me, on the other hand. . .I gulped. Maybe I could read mine.

"Sure. That would be fine." My mouth formed the words but my heart lurched. The compatibility questionnaire burned in my hand. Maybe it would reveal more surprises than I had bargained for.

After that, the pastor took notes about dates and members of the wedding party. When we left his office, people had gathered for the Wednesday night potluck dinner.

The prayer service that followed put all my thoughts about murder and burglaries and the wedding behind, although lots of people prayed that the police would have the murderer in custody soon. Afterward, I caught up with Suzanne to make arrangements for tomorrow.

"Hey there!" Enid Waldberg, our sweet pastor's wife said. "You're just the ladies I wanted to see."

Uh-oh. I recalled Suzanne's reminder about the nursing home.

Enid's face had that determined look, bent on roping us into doing something out of the kindness of our hearts.

"Tomorrow is our monthly nursing home visit. You offered to accompany me on the next visit." She beamed at us, certain of our pleasure in doing our Christian duty.

That was before small things like blackmail, burglary, and murder had taken over my life.

"Oh, I'd love that." At least Suzanne hadn't lost her enthusiasm for the venture. She winked at me. "Research for playing the role of Martha Brewster in the play."

"Oh, yes, it would be wonderful if you could do a dramatic reading. They would enjoy that." Enid turned to me. "And Cici, perhaps you could speak about whatever you choose to wear tomorrow. It might be tactful to wear something from before 1920. Some of them might not consider the sixties as vintage years. Although you look lovely today."

Enid's sweet exterior hid a core of steel, perhaps even stronger than her husband's. After I made it home, I went to my closet in search of an outfit for tomorrow. Formal wear a lá 1913, that was the ticket. Magda had asked me to wear her pearls, and the police would return them tomorrow. I brushed my hand over the real fur trim around the neckline and hoped I wouldn't run into any animal rights activists.

For our evening's foray to the college library, though, I decided to change into jeans. My sixties outfit would stand out like Columbo's trench coat in a corporate office. In ordinary street clothes, I might pass as an older student taking classes, someone like Peppi herself, closer to my age than to Dina's.

My sister picked me up a few minutes before nine. Her student parking sticker enabled her to park closer to the library building. Her all-black attire looked like she intended to burgle valuable books. Then again, her shocking pink hair ruled out the possibility of sneaking by. Heads turned whenever she walked past. A bulging backpack sat on the rear seat.

"Doing homework?"

"I might as well while I'm there. I've got a couple of papers due before the end of the semester." She opened her hazel eyes wide. "Camouflage."

What excuse could I offer for my presence at the library?

"You're looking for a particular volume on fashion history." Dina must have read my thoughts. "You could ask Peppi to order it for you through interlibrary loan."

Another thought troubled me. "We should have told the police about our suspicions."

Pink hair flew in a dozen directions as Dina shook her

head. "They know the e-mails originated from the college. They have their own sources. We're not hiding anything." In other words, she didn't want the police to spoil our fun.

The campus parking lot loomed like a deserted playground, with only a few people around to take advantage of the amenities. I spotted half-a-dozen cars. We walked through automatic sliding doors into yesterday. In spite of recent remodeling, nothing could change the smell of book dust and the quiet chatter of library patrons.

Dina perched on a stool by a computer and began clicking keys. Doing her research, I suppose. I approached Peppi at the circulation desk and asked her about interlibrary loans.

"Yes, certainly we can arrange to get books for you." She winked at me and leaned toward me, speaking in a whisper. "Only a few more minutes until the zero hour." She nodded at the wall clock, which read 9:25.

"How are we going to do this?" Steno pad in hand, Dina was ready to record the story.

We looked at each other.

"There are only a few people left," Peppi said. "I thought we would just wander around and see who's at the computers."

"Spy on them." Dina grinned in anticipation.

"Before we do anything, I'm going to call Frances. I still think we need to let her know." I dug my cell phone out of my purse and dialed her number.

From a distant corner of the library, I heard an answering buzz.

11

From: Frances Waller (Funnygirl@ggcc.net)
Date: Wednesday, April 23, 9:39 PM
To: Cord Grace (cgrace.Circle_G@ggcoc.net)
Subject: Secret?

I came here straight from church. A couple of people asked me where I was on Sunday. How long. . .

Wednesday, April 23

The ringing stopped after one buzz.

"Cici, what's up?" Frances spoke into my ear.

Dina tiptoed down the aisles and motioned for me to follow.

"I, uh, dialed your number by mistake." I knew I sounded lame. Why did my stock of small talk disappear when I needed it most? I snapped the phone shut and followed Dina down the aisle, Peppi a few steps ahead of me.

We reached the end of the aisles and walked into the computer room, empty except for one lone figure. Frances sat in front of a monitor, guilty surprise written all over her face.

Frances—the blackmailer? My mind refused to wrap itself around that idea.

Peppi stepped forward. "Can I help you with anything? You seem caught up in your research."

The surprise faded from Frances's eyes, although high

color remained in her cheeks. "You're not here about my 'research.' Not with those two along." She leveled her gaze at me, silently reminding me of the way I had dragged the police into our reenactment of Penn Hardy's murder last fall.

With that look, I knew she couldn't be the blackmailer, in spite of the suspicious timing.

Dina circled behind Frances during the conversation. She peered at the screen and let out a whoop of laughter. Peppi gave her a disapproving look, and she silenced her mirth.

"Funny girl? To Cord? Cord Grace?"

The color that had begun to fade in Frances's cheeks surged tomato red again. "Is there somewhere we can speak privately?"

"The staff room," Peppi offered. We didn't speak as we walked down the aisle and behind the circulation desk, giggles escaping Dina every few seconds.

Three of us sat on one side of a long table, across from Frances. I wondered how she felt being on the other side of an investigation.

"I come to the library for *privacy*." Frances looked at her fingers, twined together in front of her. "I have homework to do. I've started taking college classes."

"I've noticed that you're here every night. After 9:30," Peppi said.

"Yes, I come after play practice or after my shift ends." Frances lifted her head, understanding flitting across her features. "After 9:30. You mean—you thought I might be Elsie Holland?"

"We thought the person who used the same library computer every night at 9:35 might be Elsie Holland." I explained our reasoning.

"So you decided to investigate on your own. Again." She shook her head at me.

"But now we know your secret." Dina couldn't contain herself any longer. "You have to tell us. You—and Cord?" She let out a full-throated laugh.

"Why do you think it's so funny? Cord is a good man and—"

My mind put things together. The doughnut they shared at Gaynor Goodies. Frances's presence at a lot of rehearsals when she wasn't called. Her absence from church on Sunday. "You went with Cord to church last week, didn't you?" Why hadn't that made the rumor mill? Maybe because no Gaynors would be caught dead in the church where the Graces worshipped, and for once, Jessie didn't have a clue.

"We started dating about a month ago," Frances confessed. The bright red flush softened to a romantic pink. "And yes, I usually e-mail him while I'm here at night."

I wondered what kind of silliness they wrote to each other.

"Frances, I'm so happy for you. And for Cord." In fact, I thought they would make a terrific couple. But that still left the question of Elsie Holland and Jerry Burton. "But if—*since* you're not Elsie Holland—" I corrected myself "—who is? Have you noticed anyone else using the computers while you've been here?"

"No. At least not the same person every night." Frances sighed. "Ladies, you have to leave the investigating to us. The police, I mean. The blackmailer turned into a murderer when Spencer died." She had turned professional again. "We're checking out the computer angle." She pulled her soft brown hair into a ponytail. "Is there anything else you want to tell me? Any other 'facts' you've turned up?"

I thought about our total lack of success in the pawn shop hunt on Monday. "No." *I mean, we hadn't learned anything, had we?*

We said our good-byes. Frances promised to return Magda's pearls in the morning. Peppi stayed behind to close the library, so Dina and I departed. I couldn't stop smiling at the thought of Cord and Frances as a couple. I was glad that my old boyfriend hadn't pined after my engagement to another man.

Once in bed I couldn't get to sleep right away. No matter what Frances said, I felt compelled to investigate Spencer's murder. Someone had lured him to my store with malicious intent. That made it personal. I fell into a troubled sleep. I dreamed of a double wedding. During the vows, Pastor Waldberg asked, "Do you, Elsie Holland, take this man?" When I awoke on Thursday morning, I pondered on Elsie's identity again. Every door I tried led me deeper into a maze.

But I set aside sleuthing for the morning, concentrating on remodeling my store. Because of the fancy dress I had donned for the nursing home visit, I decided on ordinary bagels from Gaynor Goodies. No need to risk stray crumbs or jam on my outfit. I finished my first cup of coffee and a bagel a few minutes before nine.

A moment later, Frances Waller walked through the door, bearing a bag.

"You made it!" I lifted out Magda's pearls. They came alive in the light. "Magda begged me to wear her pearls, and today I have the perfect excuse. I'm visiting the nursing home with Enid. Will you help me get them on?"

"Sure, since Audie isn't here to do it for you." Frances grinned.

"Speaking of boyfriends—I'm so happy for you and Cord."

"I'm glad. I was afraid you might, you know, be jealous, since you used to date." Frances's gentle fingers held the necklace against the back of my neck. "I've always liked him, but he only had eyes for you. Now, though. . ." She stepped back, the pearls secured in place.

I turned around. A faint blush spread across Frances's cheeks. *She's serious.*

"He is a good man. He just wasn't the right one for me." I hugged her. "I hope things work out for the two of you."

She hugged me back, the hold expressing feelings that her words did not, and then left.

With the pearls nestled around my neck, I felt like a queen. They gave me the confidence boost I needed to take on the old ladies at the nursing home. They would pick up on any errors in clothing style that I made.

Enid and Suzanne arrived a few minutes before twelve.

"Don't you look lovely. I'm sure the ladies will enjoy hearing all about that dress," Enid said.

"Aren't those Magda's pearls?" Suzanne asked. She wore her costume from last year's production of *Much Ado About Nothing*. I wondered what bit of the play would she share with our audience?

I nodded. "Frances dropped them off this morning." I hung the CLOSED sign on the door and walked with the others to Enid's waiting van. Its spacious comfort made me wonder about investing in a larger vehicle than my little

Civic. *Easier to carry merchandise for the business.* But did the advantages outweigh the additional cost for gas? After all, I didn't have a family to haul around—at least not yet. My mind raced around the question until I realized the source of my discomfort. *Avoidance.* I didn't want to think about going to the nursing home. It reminded me of the last time I saw my grandmother. Ever since her death, I had avoided it like I might be the next to die. I prayed for peace.

When Enid parked by the front entrance, I took a deep breath, gathered my skirts, and stepped down from the van. In the foyer I paused to regain my bearings. The facility hadn't changed much in the nine years since my last visit. The wall had been repainted the same institutional green, with new and cheerful paintings. The linoleum floor looked every bit as scuffed, and the air, if anything, seemed even mustier in spite of a fresh breeze blowing through opened windows.

Enid touched my arm. "The community room is this way." We walked down a short hallway, with glimpses into rooms made cheerful with colorful afghans and fresh flowers. Someone put effort into making the residents' homes away from home pleasant.

We rounded a corner and walked into a room full of people in everything from Sunday dress and walkers to pajamas and wheelchairs. Our audience. Enid toured the room, introducing Suzanne and me to every person present. Many of the names and faces were familiar to me from the days they still lived at home. Guilt for neglecting them when they dropped out of sight replaced my previous unease.

Enid stopped in front of a lady with titian-dyed hair.

"Mrs. Lambert. I'd like for you to meet Suzanne Jay and Cecilia Wilde."

Lambert? Why did that name ring a bell?

Mrs. Lambert fixed gimlet eyes on me. She reached out a gnarled hand toward my neck. I stepped back, frightened by the implied threat.

"Why are you wearing my pearls?"

"I'm sorry?" I stammered. "Magda Grace Mallory gave me these pearls."

"That one." Venom laced Mrs. Lambert's voice. "I don't understand why my son ever became involved with that harlot."

Harlot? Was the old lady confusing Magda with someone else?

"Just ignore her," Enid whispered in my ear and tugged me to the next resident.

Senility, I supposed. She must have owned a string of pearls once upon a time and thought they were hers.

After that little episode, the rest of the visit went fine. Enid presented a short devotion. They interacted with my presentation of fashion tips and diary excerpts from the original Grace Gulch Ladies Society. Several of them remembered pictures and stories their mothers had shared with them.

But Suzanne was the hit of the day, with her monologue that began, "What fire is in mine ears?" *Taming my wild heart to thy loving hand.* What beautiful words. How could I ever write my own wedding vows? Shakespeare, I was not.

Thinking of wedding vows reminded me that I needed to start on the compatibility questionnaire that the pastor had given us. I worked on it before rehearsal. I raced through the first few questions, rating things like "same spiritual beliefs" and "sense of humor" a solid "10". But others gave me pause. Beyond American middle class, we did not share a common background. I had only met his parents once; how could I know if I hoped Audie would resemble them as he aged? I jotted down the first number that jumped into my mind.

Audie and I shared a hurried dinner at my house before heading to the theater. I mentioned Mrs. Lambert's strange reaction to Magda's pearls.

"I wonder if she's related to Peppi. She's a Lambert, too."

"You know the area families better than I do. I wouldn't worry about what she said. It sounds like she's gaga." Audie shrugged it off. "You know what Wilde said about being old?"

"Tell me." I could use a laugh.

"'I am not young enough to know everything.' The poor old thing has probably forgotten half of what she knew once upon a time."

What she might have forgotten was what frightened me.

12

From: Jerry Burton (cbtrotter@redbud.net)
Date: Wednesday, April 23, 9:47 PM
To: Magda Mallory (mgmallory@ggcoc.net)
Subject: Pearls

A recent edition of the Grace Gulch Herald
*reported that you are donating vintage pearls for
use in the upcoming production of* Arsenic and
Old Lace. *The same pearls were discovered at
Victor Spencer's murder scene.*

*Are you acting out of benevolence—or do you
want to get rid of unwanted evidence?*

I know what happened forty years ago.

*Expect further communication from me on the
subject.*

Thursday, April 24

What Mrs. Lambert knows isn't the problem." I put
on a good face. "The pearls reminded me that I
haven't made any progress on the murder. With your
permission I want to check your files tonight. See if I've
missed something about Spencer."

Audie nodded. "Sure. But there's something—"

Gene arrived at that moment, little Bobo dashing ahead of him.

Chagrin darkened Gene's good looks. "I'm sorry about the scene the other night. I'd still like to be in the play, if you'll have me."

Audie grunted. Although he didn't say so, Gene's accusations had stung. But the theater needed all the volunteers it could get, and Audie couldn't afford to offend the son of his patron. Besides, Gene brought out all the comic creepiness of the doctor.

A smile lit Audie's face, his eyes shading toward cerulean blue. "Welcome back, Gene. I'm glad to have you."

Bobo yipped his pleasure.

Everybody came to rehearsal that night and settled down to work as if the disaster on Tuesday night had never happened. I put together ice water and tea, but instead of watching the play, I slipped back to the office. I figured that I had at least an hour before the first break, and I wanted to learn as much as possible about Vic Spencer.

Memorabilia crammed the office. I skimmed through scripts, set designs, playbills arranged in a haphazard order on the desktop. Organization wasn't Audie's strong point. A single two-drawer file cabinet held all the office records for the theater. However, I didn't find a folder labeled "Spencer, Victor" or a more general label "personnel." I pulled out files one at a time, finally locating Spencer in the section marked "Expenses." The record contained scant information: his address, social security number, a photo of his driver's license. Nothing that I didn't already know. I decided to make a copy of the driver's license photo in case we needed to show it around.

Frustrated, I turned to organizing Audie's desk while

I was there. He wouldn't mind, and something else about Spencer might come to light. I grabbed a pile of pages from the printer, about half as high as a ream of paper. A quick glance told me most of it could be discarded: multiple copies of the same rehearsal schedule and cast changes. I would cut it into scrap paper as I went. Maybe I should spend time in here after every rehearsal and help Audie out. *Then again, this is his job!* I reminded myself. At least his mind was organized, and he could always lay his hands on what he needed.

I had made my way through a third of the pile when words jumped off the page. *I know your secret.* I had found a copy of the same e-mail that Spencer held in his hand.

After that, I found copies of other e-mails I had heard about, plus a few that no one had mentioned. The word *pearls* in the subject line on one page caught my attention.

"I know what happened forty years ago," it read. I didn't see how ancient history connected with Magda's pearls at all. It probably didn't, only the same overactive imagination that suspected foul play behind every curtain. I read the e-mail again. This one was addressed to Magda, from Jerry Burton.

Why did Audie have e-mails from both Jerry Burton and Elsie Holland on his desk? Could he be—? *No, of course not.* But if not Audie, then who? I remembered that Audie had started to tell me something when Gene arrived. Maybe he wanted to tell me about these messages.

Were Jerry and Elsie two different people or the same person writing under two different names? The presence of the notes in Audie's office suggested that the same person had access to the community college library and the theater office. Who was it? Were all the blackmail targets involved with the theater? I shook my head; I knew better. Jessie had received an e-mail from Elsie Holland. And had something happened forty years ago that could support blackmail? Magda and Mayor Ron had both been adults at that time; maybe they could shed light on the puzzle.

The questions required some thinking. I might assume that Vic Spencer had blackmailed several victims, and one of them had killed him, except that the threats had continued after his death. I rummaged through the prop shelves and found one of Dina's steno pads.

"What's up?"

As soft as Audie's voice was, it still made me jump out of my seat. I looked at the clock: half-past eight. I spent more time contemplating the blackmail notes than I expected. "I'm sorry. Do you need more water? Tea?"

Audie shook his head. "I let them go early." He put his arms around my shoulders. "What's the matter? You're as jumpy as a mouse running away from a cat." He saw the papers on the desk. "You found the e-mails, I see."

"How long have you known about them?" I used the direct approach.

"I was checking the trash can on my desktop screen before deleting them permanently. These e-mails were in the trash can. I printed them out and gave them to the police." He flashed a smile. "I kept a copy for myself, naturally."

Why didn't you tell me?

"I intended to tell you about them tonight."

I took a deep breath. "Whoever did this must have access to your office. When you're not here, obviously. So it's someone who knows the theater personnel and schedule."

"It's someone we know, and know well."

I voiced the question that must be on both our minds. "What do you think the forty-year-old secret refers to? Do you think it's connected to Spencer's murder?" I half expected Audie to come out with an Oscar Wilde quip, but he didn't. Not this time.

"We know he didn't have any secrets from that long ago. He wasn't born yet."

"He might have heard about it, though. I finally figured out where I remembered him from. He was a few years ahead of Jenna in school. He's been around off and on for years."

"There could be two blackmailers." Audie tapped the papers with a slender finger. "Spencer was threatening someone else, but then he was caught."

We looked at each other for a long moment.

"The more I learn, the muddier everything gets." My mind spun. "First we were looking for a murderer. Then a thief. Then maybe a pair of thieves. And now maybe a pair of blackmailers. Is that one person, two—or five? And who?" I pointed to the computer. "I understand that there are experts who can dig into a computer's memory and see what was written by whom and when, but I don't know how to do that. And—"

"I asked the chief about that. He said not to worry. He seems to think they already have their primary suspect."

"Who?" Although I suspected I knew the answer.

"Me. The only reason they haven't arrested me is that they can't figure out a motive, and so far there's no physical evidence. Besides, Magda gave me a good alibi."

When had Audie spoken with the police without me? Did he go without an attorney? That was the action of an innocent man; couldn't they see that?

"But I do know who we have to talk to first." Determination shaded Audie's eyes a midnight blue. "Magda. She's mentioned by name in the letters." His voice wobbled just a tad. "And she also might know what happened forty years ago."

"Isn't there another way?" A discussion about possible blackmail couldn't help the ongoing contract negotiations.

"Not if we want to get to the bottom of this. 'The only thing worse than being talked about is not being talked about.'" The Wilde quote only brought a faint smile to his lips. "We can't afford to keep quiet about this. And Magda deserves to know what's going on in her theater." He trained his eyes on me while he picked up the phone and called Magda. She agreed to let us come right over.

"She's one tough old lady." I grabbed the chinchilla boa I had worn from work to ward off the evening chill. "This makes the second time this week we've shown up on her doorstep late at night."

Audie grunted, and I remembered that he had also been at Magda's house the night of the murder. His car could probably drive there without him steering the wheel.

Magda met us at the door. "Come in." Her face lit up when she saw me. "You're wearing the pearls! They look lovely on you."

Her comment reminded me of my encounter with the old lady at the nursing home. Well, Mrs. Lambert was senile, nothing more.

Magda led us to the same drawing room where she entertained us two nights before. "I missed you at rehearsal tonight. You're our most faithful audience."

"I'm sorry, I got involved in Audie's office and lost track of the time."

Magda bustled away to the kitchen before I could explain what had kept me busy for the evening—the reason for our visit. She returned with a tea tray.

"I know you avoid caffeine at night. Very wise of you. This is raspberry tea. Herbal." She poured it into dainty china cups with the elegance of a duchess and at last sat back in her chair.

"Are you concerned about the trust? I signed the papers at Lauren's office this morning." Niceties completed, she prepared to discuss business.

"That's not it." Audie paused, the tea cup poised midair. "Although let me thank you again for your thoughtfulness and foresight. It is a gift to the entire community of Grace Gulch, indeed, all of Oklahoma—and especially to me." If Audie ever decided to give up the theater, he could have a splendid career in politics. Join a distinguished line of former actors that included Reagan and Schwarzenegger.

He paused and looked at me for help. Sometimes even politicians struggled to find the right words.

I could think of no way to sugarcoat the subject we needed to ask Magda about. Since someone had to bring it up, it might as well be me. She didn't pay my salary.

I drew a deep breath, as deep as I could with my diaphragm constricted by the corset required for the day's costume. "I was in the office during the rehearsal tonight looking for information about the murder victim in the files."

"Vic Spencer. Yes, I engaged his services for the theater." Magda nodded. Her voice remained polite, but she must have wondered about the reason for our late night visit. "Did you learn anything of interest?"

"Not exactly." I couldn't tell her about the blackmail note we had seen in Spencer's hand. The police hadn't released that information yet. "I found something that may concern you, though."

Audie nodded, and I unrolled the blackmail notes that I had found. We had decided to show her everything. It was her theater, after all.

Looking at the papers as I smoothed them, I said, "Someone involved with the MGM has been threatening people. Has anyone. . .written to you?"

"Let me see what you have." Magda set her cup on the tray and reached for the papers.

No one spoke while she perused the pages once, twice, three times. Audie's spoon clinked against the china cup when he added sugar to his tea. In the absolute silence of the room, it sounded as loud as a dinner bell. I lifted the cup to my lips and sniffed it, hoping the scent might slow down my racing nerves.

If Grace Gulch had royalty, Magda Grace Mallory was it. Always in control, she exuded a regal, commanding presence. Even when Gene made a scene at rehearsal the other night, she left in style.

Her royal manner failed her tonight. Her lips tightened at the corners, then trembled. Her face paled as if an unseen hand had wiped the makeup from her face and shown its true pallor. Her breath came in quick, sharp gasps.

"I didn't think anyone else knew the story. At least not until I read the e-mail in my inbox." She spoke in a voice so low she could have been talking to herself. She straightened her shoulders and looked up. Still pale, the uncertainty had vanished. "The truth will come out as soon as the terms of my will become known. In light of these threats, I think—I think you need to know now." Bright spots appeared in her cheeks. "You might not guess it to look at me now, but I was a wild, headstrong girl. Almost forty years ago, I left a wonderful young man behind in Grace Gulch and headed to Chicago to seek my fame and fortune in the theater."

Audie stirred beside me.

"Yes, I was interested in the theater, even back then. I was naïve enough to believe the casting couch would guarantee my success."

I set down my cup of tea before I dropped it.

"You needn't be so shocked." A small, sad smile tugged at Magda's mouth. "I've asked God to forgive me, and I know He has. It was all over a long time ago." Her eyes took on a dreamy look. "Of course the inevitable happened. I got pregnant, gave birth, and gave the child up for adoption. I met my dear Matthew when I came home, and later we married. When Gene came along, I suppose I spoiled him, trying to make up for the child I had given away."

13

From: Elsie Holland (Snoozeulose@ggcc.com)
Date: Wednesday, April 23, 9:50 PM
To: Lauren Packer (LPacker@ggcoc.net)
Subject: Partner in crime?

> *Gossip suggests that you knew murder victim Vic Spencer from college.*

> *Did something happen eighteen years ago that gave you reason to kill him?*

> *Expect further communication from me on the subject.*

Thursday, April 24

Magda had a child out of wedlock? And gave him or her away for adoption almost forty years ago? My mind groped toward the truth.

Audie got there ahead of me. "Suzanne!" His voice vibrated with all the pent-up emotions of the night.

My mind whirled, reorganizing facts in a new configuration.

"Yes. Suzanne." The bright spots in Magda's cheeks faded and once again she looked like a well-preserved matron. "When she first contacted me, I refused to talk with her. I put that episode behind me years ago. But she was persistent, and I confess I was curious as to how my other child turned out." Her lips curled for an instant. "If she was any more. . .satisfactory. . .than Gene. If I had made the right decision in giving her away." Tears appeared in her eyes. "We began corresponding. I traveled to Chicago several times to meet with her and discovered how much alike we are, in ways both good and bad."

So that was what brought the semi-successful actress to this backwater of theater, Grace Gulch. The most fundamental reason of all: family, a desire to know and be known, to love and be loved. Maybe I was projecting, but I didn't think so.

"Since she's come to Grace Gulch, we've been able to get together more often. We've tried to be discreet. . .as you know, no easy task in this small town, but someone must have ferreted out the truth."

I hadn't heard a word, a whisper of a rumor, about Suzanne and Magda's relationship. How they had accomplished that feat of secrecy boggled my mind.

Magda didn't speak for a few moments. Her face relaxed, recapturing the innocence and beauty that must have marked her as a young woman, a wistful longing for the child she had lost and the dreams she had left behind. A delicate lilac scent wafted through the air. She was a lady, and her secret would not change my opinion of her. "You are an amazing woman." I wanted to put my arms around her, but I held back. One simply didn't hug Magda Grace Mallory.

She made a sound that was half a cough, half a laugh. "How can you say that after you know the truth about me?"

"But don't you see?" Audie pressed my hand, and I knew he shared my thoughts. "Your past makes you even more amazing. You overcame your errors in judgment. You have been a shining example of God's grace to all of us here in Grace Gulch, although we never knew why."

"Even when your own dreams fell apart, you came home and made Grace Gulch a better place to grow up in." I felt compelled to make her understand. "Thank you. For me. For all of us who grew up with music and culture because of you. People won't think less of you when they learn the truth. If anything, it will help people."

"Oh, my dear." Magda smiled, the first genuine smile I had seen on her face that night. "Thank *you*. Thank you for helping Suzanne to see the truth about our precious Lord last fall. She was headed down the same road I had already traveled, and you helped to turn her back."

"'A good man leaves an inheritance for his children's children.' Proverbs 13:22. God is proving His promise with everything that's happened with Suzanne." Audie spoke in soft tones.

"As well as a financial inheritance." Magda almost giggled. "I've added Suzanne to my will."

"We still have a problem."

"You're right." Emotions reined in, Magda returned to business. "Who wrote the blackmail letters?"

"You don't know?" If she wanted the direct approach, I would oblige her. "Did Mr. Burton. . .or whoever it is, communicate with you further, as he threatened?"

"Why, no!" Magda brushed aside the suggestion with a wave of her hand. "Suzanne and I talked about it. She received a note from the same Burton fellow, but he hasn't written again." She rifled through the pages again, as if she would discover something she hadn't seen the first time. "We've been expecting someone to approach us ever since we received the e-mails, especially after last night." She waved her e-mail. "But you're the first to come to me."

Had we made a mistake in coming tonight? Would she think. . .

"We had nothing to do with the e-mails." The words tumbled from my mouth.

"Of course not, dear." Magda spoke with such sincerity that I couldn't doubt her.

I loved her more than ever for her assumption of our innocence. "But who? Why?"

"It has to be someone connected with the theater." Magda echoed Audie's and my conclusion. "That means it's someone we know. Half of the cast are members of my family. Oh, dear." Magda's composure threatened to slip again.

"There are some characters that don't belong to the Grace family." But not many, when I thought about it. Even Lauren was Magda's lawyer. Peppi and Frances had only minor roles. I giggled. "Maybe we could blame it on Chief Reiner and get rid of him. He's in the play."

"Now, Cici." Audie's smile nullified his reprimand.

"Perhaps the place to start is to determine who might know that Suzanne is my daughter. That's an even smaller circle than the theater group."

"Suzanne? Your *daughter*?"

Gene Mallory's bulk filled the door to the drawing room. None of us had heard him enter. How much of our conversation had he overheard?

"Oh, Gene. I never wanted you to find out this way." Magda's aplomb vanished, and her voice rose in a wail.

"Suzanne is your daughter? No wonder you're changing your will. You never loved me." He crossed the room and towered over Magda in her chair. "I'll tell you this much. I'd rather see both of you dead than for you to leave any of the Mallory money to that woman."

Magda sat straight. "Cici, Audie, dear, perhaps you should leave."

We complied. That mother-son conversation needed privacy. If Gene's reaction suggested the response Magda could expect from the rest of Grace Gulch, no wonder she had kept her past a secret for all these years.

Audie escorted me home. I couldn't get Gene's words out of my mind. By the time I prepped my dress for washing—the long day had taken its toll on the beautiful fabric—and chosen another blouse to wear with Wednesday's gypsy skirt—the hour hand reached eleven. I should have been exhausted but my mind refused to stop whirling.

Suzanne was Magda's child, born out of wedlock. Someone knew and threatened both of them. The discovery infuriated Gene. He threatened his mother and his sister. And did any of it tie into Spencer's murder? The fact that they both received blackmail notes from the same person—whoever Jerry Burton was—suggested they did. But I couldn't see the connection between Spencer's probable thievery and Magda's secret past.

Who was Jerry Burton? Who was Elsie Holland? Could they be the same person? I didn't want it to be someone I knew and cared about. I took out the list that I had started in the office. Maybe if I could organize my thoughts, I could get to sleep.

I forced personal feeling aside and created a page for each person connected to the theater—even Audie, although my fingers trembled as I penned his name. I wanted it all spelled out to put the police's suspicions to rest when the time came. I also needed to explain any connection to the college.

Audie Howe. I listed all relevant details, circling his alibi. Not that I thought, even for a nanosecond, that Audie could be guilty of blackmail or murder. But I had to include the director with people in the theater. In any case, I knew he must be innocent, and his alibi should go a long way toward convincing hardheaded Chief Reiner. I started to tear the page out of the notebook, but something stopped me. Maybe later I would see a connection to someone else.

The second name on my list: *Magda Grace Mallory.* I wasn't sure about her connection with the college; she might be on the board of directors. The blackmail threat she received was based on the truth of her relationship to Suzanne. Audie's words when we first heard about the e-mails came back to me. "*Sooner or later, Elsie will hit too close to the truth, and someone may decide to retaliate.*" Not Magda. I couldn't imagine Magda hurting a flea.

Suzanne Jay: Did she have an alibi? In fact, I didn't know the alibi for almost anyone on the list.

Lauren Packer: Did he engage Spencer's services? They were about the same age. Did they know each other before the janitor's arrival in town? As Magda's lawyer, Packer might know her secrets.

Mayor Ron: As mayor, he was de facto director of the college, and as Magda's brother, he might have known her secret. He was rumored to have received e-mail from Elsie Holland.

Cord Grace: I could think of nothing new about my old friend, except the need to establish his alibi—probably Gene.

Gene Mallory: He was also rumored to have received e-mail from Elsie Holland. Because of his wild youth and unproductive adult life, Magda was pressing him to change.

Who else? One name jumped to mind, although I knew she was innocent.

Dina Wilde: I considered my sister without prejudice. Could she have uncovered information behind the e-mails? She was a reporter, after all. Still, could I envision her as a blackmailer? No, absolutely not.

I added a few more names to the list, although they had less significant roles in the play. Two of them also had connections to the college.

Peppi Lambert: She was from Chicago, as were Suzanne and Audie. Did they know each other in the past? Was she related to the lady in the nursing home?

Frances Waller: She was a police officer who knew more than could be proved about the people of Grace Gulch. I hated to admit it, but Frances remained a strong candidate for Elsie Holland when I added her nightly presence at the library into consideration.

I started to create a page for the chief. After all, he was also a cast member. But I was tuckered out, and I really couldn't envision him as a blackmailer or a murderer. How could someone who upheld even the silliest laws commit murder?

Had I accomplished anything with my musing? I had identified a number of questions. Tomorrow I would seek answers.

14

From: Elsie Holland (Snoozeulose@ggcc.com)
Date: Thursday, April 24, 9:08 PM
To: Cici Wilde (Cici's_Vintage_Clothing@ggcoc.net)
Subject: Retire the trench coat

*While your store has been closed, you have
been making the rounds of the county, asking
questions.*

*If you know what is good for you, you will stop
pestering old ladies and retire the trench coat.*

Friday, April 25

On Friday morning I paid for my late night musings
by sleeping late and skipping breakfast. I walked into
Gaynor Goodies and ordered two double shot espressos—
one to drink now and one for later. I needed something to
wake me up; I also added a breakfast croissant.

In between arranging merchandise for reopening,
I checked with the college. The board of directors did
include both the mayor and Magda; and Lauren taught
an introduction to law class every spring semester.

Three busy hours later, Audie bounced into the store,
bringing my favorite turkey and cranberry salad sandwich
from The Gulch. He looked well-rested. I had awakened
from my morning stupor, as well, and determined to ask

him about his surprises. I wouldn't tell him about his appearance on my list of suspects. No need to trouble those waters.

Audie reached out and brushed his fingers against my face. "You look tired. Are you worried about what we found out last night?"

His concern almost melted my determination to ask about the surprises. Almost.

"I'll be okay." I shook away his concern. "But I do want to ask you something." I bit into the sandwich, swallowed, and plunged ahead. "How long have you known about the Center for the Arts and the trust fund? Was that your surprise? Or is it something else?"

Audie raised an eyebrow. "So you agree with Wilde that 'It is better to have a permanent income than to be fascinating'?"

Argh. Trust Audie to sidetrack a discussion with a quote from Oscar Wilde. "What, do you think that having secrets makes you fascinating?"

Mischief flashed in Audie's sapphire eyes. "I like to think so. Come on, part of what you love about me is that I'm not from Grace Gulch. You don't know everything about me and my family since the land run." He leaned close enough to kiss me. "And we have a lifetime to learn everything about each other."

Bingo. Part of Audie's attraction for me—as well as part of my uncertainty—stemmed from his newness. I knew I loved him, and I believed that God had brought him into my life. My thoughts flashed to that compatibility test and hoped it didn't reveal any big problems. I felt my cheeks heating.

He drew back and let me regain my bearings for a

moment. "To answer your question directly, I didn't know about the trust fund before you did, but I did know about the Center for the Arts. There is more I want to tell you, but I need you to trust me a little while longer. I'll tell you soon. As soon as a couple more pieces fall into place."

"Do you intend to do this when we're married?"

"Do what?" Audie finished his sandwich—tuna salad—and opened up a brownie wrapped in cellophane. He broke it and offered half to me.

"Keep all the facts to yourself until you've decided what you want to do?"

This wasn't 1891, when town founder Bob Grace told his fiancée that he planned to take part in the next land run without asking her opinion. In the twenty-first century, women expected to have a say in family matters.

"Of course not." Audie seemed surprised. "But I don't even know the facts yet. Just pray for me, okay? I promise that I'll tell you soon. Maybe even before we finish that compatibility questionnaire." He wiggled his eyebrows. "We don't want to flunk the test."

I giggled. I could never stay frustrated at Audie for long, and I did trust him.

After we finished eating, I brought up the subject of the investigation. "I want to talk with Magda again, this time about Spencer. I have the feeling that she knows more about him than she's told us."

"That sounds like a good idea." Audie nodded. "She might know something about his past that would throw light on his murder." He gathered the trash and threw it away. "Of course, if she knows anything, she's already told the police."

"She hasn't summoned the chief for an interview.

Jessie would have spread the word." I grinned. "Still, I want to see her again."

In the end, I decided to call. I explained what I wanted, and she suggested that we meet fifteen minutes before the scheduled rehearsal. After a quiet supper at home, I headed for the theater and brought Magda's pearls with me, at Audie's request. He wanted to practice with them at the next couple of rehearsals. I was fingering the necklace when she walked into the office. Always regal, she now also looked serene. Maybe revealing her secrets to us had done that for her.

Magda accepted decaf coffee. The hefty mug looked incongruous in her delicate hands. "I thought about Mr. Spencer on the way over. I wish I could help you, but I don't know much more about the poor man than what he wrote on his job application. We needed a reliable cleaning crew, and when Lauren recommended Mr. Spencer's services so highly, I decided to hire him."

I hoped Magda's trust in her lawyer wasn't misplaced. I tried to think what else Magda might know about the janitor. "Did you know his family? They used to live in Grace Gulch."

Magda shrugged her thin shoulders. "Not well. Lauren mentioned going to school with Mr. Spencer, although I had the impression that he was referring to college."

Why would a college graduate choose janitorial work as a profession? Maybe it was profitable. Anything was possible. But something else bothered me.

"That's right, Lauren Packer recommended Spencer."

"Yes, and his name came up in other places, as well. I believe Ron mentioned him. In fact, the city council is looking for a replacement. City hall can't lose its sparkle, you know."

Magda continued in the same vein, talking about the image of Grace Gulch and how important it was to give visitors a good impression of a vibrant historic community and not a dirty backwater ghost town. I agreed, but tonight my mind wandered elsewhere.

Lauren Packer had recommended Victor Spencer to Magda. Why? What had caused a friendship to spring up between a janitor and Grace Gulch's primary estate lawyer? What school had the two men attended together? How long had they known each other? I ticked off questions to add to my notebook.

The clock in the office chimed seven—time for rehearsal. Before Magda left the room, she spoke again. "There is something else that I want to discuss with you. Please meet me in the office during the break."

Suzanne cornered me in the hallway. "Magda told me you found out about. . .us." She whispered and then hugged me. "I'm glad you know."

"I'm so happy for you." I meant it.

We made our way to the stage. Gene arrived at the last minute, carrying Bobo in his arms. He spat out his lines during his scene with Suzanne and Magda. The cast loved it. In this case, life imitated art and added realism to his performance. He left as soon as they finished.

Now that I knew the truth about Suzanne and Magda, I wondered why others hadn't guessed. Audie had paired them as sisters not only because of their acting ability, but also because of their resemblance. All the rest of the Brewsters in the play—crazy Teddy and sinister Jonathan—were portrayed by Graces. (The hero, Mortimer Brewster, played by Lauren Packer, learned he was adopted, and so he didn't count.) No wonder they made such a believable, if dysfunctional, family. Audie figured that stage makeup would mask the twenty-year age difference between the two actresses.

When they discussed where to bury their latest victim, even their voices sounded alike. Magda's older, softer alto echoed Suzanne's strong soprano.

But someone *had* guessed the truth, and tried blackmail—almost certainly one of the people in the theater that night. I watched the other actors, hoping to catch someone studying Magda or Suzanne. No one acted in a suspicious manner.

I made sure I had plenty of cold drinks on hand—I had taken a break from making tea and instead bought a variety of two-liter sodas. As promised, Magda met me in the office as soon as Audie called a halt to rehearsal.

"I have a marvelous idea." She sounded as excitable as Abby Brewster.

"It will only be a matter of time before people learn about my relationship with Suzanne."

Did she suspect I would gossip about her secret? "I would never—"

"Of course not. But someone else out there knows the truth and, well, we can't be sure when the grapevine will learn about it." She patted my hand. "Don't worry about me. It will be a relief for the truth to finally be told." She straightened her back, once again the regal matron of the theater. "Rather than waiting for more rumors to spread, I want to make the announcement myself. Suzanne agrees with me. The *Herald* will be interested in the story, don't you agree?"

I guessed Magda's intentions.

"Perhaps Dina can interview me. I've seen her work

at the theater; she's a levelheaded young woman. I'd rather she write the story than that new editor. Do you think she'll agree to speak with me?"

"Wow." What an opportunity for my sister. If Hardy, the previous owner of the *Herald*, were still alive, Magda would have asked him. They were distant cousins, after all. "I know she'd want to talk with you. And she may want to drag Peppi along, since she's interning at the paper."

"Very well. I'll talk with both of them."

I hesitated, uncertain whether to add more, but decided to plunge ahead. "I think you're wise to reveal the truth about Suzanne."

"All the Gaynors will be rejoicing." Magda looked resigned.

"Perhaps. But most people will admire the way you handled a difficult situation."

Behind Magda, I saw a flicker of movement. Perhaps someone needed to get more ice or soda from the refrigerator. Or perhaps someone had passed by the door when we discussed the specifics about Suzanne.

If so—the promised interview would come one day too late.

15

From: Jerry Burton (cbtrotter@redbud.net)
Date: Friday, April 25, 9:36 PM
To: Magda Mallory (mgmallory@ggcoc.net)
Subject: Hidden secrets

The truth will come out. You are like the religious leaders that Jesus accused of being white-washed sepulchers.

I not only know what happened forty years ago; I know what happened eighteen years ago.

Expect to see me soon.

Saturday, April 26

When I stopped by Gaynor Goodies on Saturday morning, I wondered if Jessie would greet me with questions about Suzanne and Magda.

Yesterday, Jessie had ribbed me about the incident with Mrs. Lambert at the nursing home. The day before, she had asked how the premarital counseling session had gone with the pastor. She also admired Magda's pearls and tried to pry more information out of me. I was wearing the pearls, of course. I tried to be circumspect in my answers—anything told to Jessie would soon be known town-wide.

Today she didn't say much of anything. She didn't mention Magda at all or anyone else involved in the play. For one day I had not provided fodder for the town gossip mill, and that suited me fine.

I spent the morning planning my next window display. I decided against putting the '30s material back out; why remind potential customers of mayhem and murder every time they walked by?

Instead I would proceed to the next decade, the war years. I had located several well-preserved women's uniforms from each branch of service: WACS, WAVES, SPARS, WASP. I was partial to the uniforms of the Cadet Nurse Program, which was supervised by the Public Health Service. My father's mother had worn the brown army-style jacket—khaki blouse, skirt, and tie—with pride.

For my window, however, I decided to highlight native Oklahoman Marjorie Dresbach. After her meeting with Jacqueline Cochran, the driving force behind the WASPs, Marjorie served at Spence Field in Moultrie, Georgia. I had the perfect WASP uniform to go with her life story.

By lunchtime I had sketched out the display and penned placards for the featured items. I went through my back storeroom to locate other items from the '40s. I wouldn't actually sell the uniforms; that seemed like a sacrilege to the women who defended our country so bravely. But I expected to turn a tidy profit on a large inventory that harkened back to America's "greatest generation."

I was dressing my mannequin in a bomber jacket and slacks when Dina and Peppi entered.

"Bologna today." Dina held up a brown paper sack. "Hope you don't mind."

I would have eaten peanut butter and jelly if Dina brought it. She rarely provided lunch. The girls' arrival reminded me of Magda's decision to reveal all about Suzanne. For a few hours, I had immersed myself completely in the heroics of the war years and forgotten my own personal quest for answers. Who killed Vic Spencer? Who was burglarizing Lincoln County? And who was sending threatening e-mails to the people of Grace Gulch? I was no closer to an answer than I was a week ago, when Audie discovered Spencer's body.

"You left me a message. Said it was urgent. What's up? Do you want our help investigating again?" Today Dina wore a pink-and-white checked button-down shirt, untucked, of course. It matched her hair. Peppi, in her blue-and-lavender plaid big shirt, looked almost normal.

"No, it has nothing to do with the murder."

"Blackmail, then." Dina grinned.

"What would you say if I told you that Magda Grace Mallory wants both of you to interview her?"

"Magda? That's awesome!" Dina zipped out a date book with two cute kittens on the cover. "When? And what's the occasion?" She stopped, her pen poised in mid-air. "Oh, wait a minute, this isn't about the Center for the Arts, is it? That's old news."

"No. It's. . .personal."

"Maybe she's going to get married," Peppi suggested with a giggle.

"Did we miss a birthday or something?" Dina thumbed through her date book. Magda could command a community-wide celebration any time she wanted to. Of course she rarely did, and never for herself, which made us love her all the more. "Nah. Her birthday's in August."

My little sister never failed to amaze me. She had Magda's birthday at her fingertips, literally.

"Can you two keep a secret?" I wasn't sure how much I should tell them.

"Reporters never reveal their sources." Peppi spouted journalism 101.

"Well, it's a secret until you talk with Magda and get the details."

"Magda has a secret," Dina said in the same singsong voice she used when she crept behind me and Cord— back when we dated in high school—and said "Cici has a boyfriend." Dina smirked. "Do tell."

I couldn't resist. They would know all about it soon enough. "Well, Magda wants to talk to you about a child she gave birth to."

"Gene?" Dina scoffed. "He's no story."

"No, not Gene. A baby born before Magda was married."

"Magda had a child out of wedlock?"

Peppi's lack of surprise reminded me of Mrs. Lambert's accusation, but before I could ask about it, Dina interrupted.

"How come we didn't know about this already?" Dina, the Grace Gulch native, wanted to know. "And who is it? Someone we know?"

"Magda will tell you the rest." I waved my hands. "She'll see you at half past four this afternoon if that works for you."

"If! I would skip a final to get a story like this." Dina jumped to her feet, ready to head over to Magda's house at that moment.

"I'm coming with you when you go." I wanted to hear the details firsthand.

Peppi's mouth opened in a perfect oval. "You're not a reporter."

"No. But Magda is my friend. I want to offer my support."

We arranged to meet at the store at quarter past four and head over to the Mallory mansion together. The two girls returned at the appointed hour with a backpack full of reporter accessories: recorder, spare batteries and tapes, camera, even the faithful steno notebook. Dina attempted to pry more information out of me during the five-minute drive.

"The child must have been born when Magda was away. You know, after high school? When she supposedly went off to seek fame and fortune in the theater."

I shook my head. "You won't get it out of me that easily."

Since Magda had set the time of our appointment, I expected her to greet us at the door. Instead we found a three-by-five index card taped to the door which read, *If I don't answer your knock, please enter. I can't hear when I'm at the back of the house. The door isn't locked.*

I knocked once. Dina knocked a second time and then opened the door. "Magda?"

I repeated her name. Through the arch to the drawing room, I saw that Magda had prepared for company. A pitcher of iced tea waited on a mirrored serving tray.

"Magda?" Dina moved past me into the house, Peppi following close behind. We poked our heads through every open doorway, calling out her name. I paused by the bathroom and, feeling a bit silly, laid my ear against the door. She might be too much of a lady to answer from that location. No sounds emerged, however.

Dina headed for the back of the house, where the kitchen was located. The scream that followed would have done justice to a horror film—pure terror and surprise and fright.

Peppi ran down the hallway ahead of me. The two of us peered over Dina's shoulder where we stood at the door.

First, I noticed the three-inch high heels that Magda loved to wear through long hours of rehearsal. My eyes traced her form from stocking-encased legs past a pink silk dress. Last of all, I forced myself to look at her face, an unrecognizable, ugly shade of blue. I considered checking her pulse. *No.* I shuddered. She couldn't possibly be alive.

Small white objects were scattered across the floor, as if a turtle had laid her eggs in the kitchen. I bent forward to get a closer look—pearls. The broken strand hung from Magda's neck. Fearful that I would get sick, I pulled back and punched 9-1-1 into my cell phone.

"What is the nature of your emergency?"

What should I say? I didn't want to announce Magda's death over airwaves that anyone with a police scanner could hear.

"Uh. This is Cici Wilde. We need help at Magda Grace Mallory's house. It's at the—"

"I have the address. Someone will be there soon." A slight tremor in the dispatcher's voice suggested the questions that must be running through her mind.

Dina recovered from her shock enough to retrieve her camera from her backpack. Her reporter instincts were kicking in.

"Don't go in the room," I cautioned her.

"Someone needs to check for a pulse." She ignored

me and knelt by the still body. In a steady voice she whispered, "She's dead." She backed up a few feet and snapped a picture.

It was time to back out of big-sister mode. Dina knew what to do. On the other hand, a white-faced Peppi had taken a single step back from the doorway.

"Come with me." I placed my arm around the young woman's shoulders and led her back to the drawing room. The drink tray Magda had prepared for her guests seemed like the perfect antidote to shock. The police wouldn't object, would they? This room wasn't part of the crime scene. The murderer would not have stopped to grab a drink on the way out the door. I poured three glasses of tea. After a minute, Dina joined us. Peppi's face had regained a bit of its normal color when the front doorbell rang and then opened.

"Cici?" Frances Waller had responded to the call. An ambulance careened around the corner.

"We're in here." I wiped my mouth with a napkin and stood up.

She took in the scene with a glance—the three of us, drinking tea without the services of a hostess. "What happened?"

I steeled myself. "She's. . .back there."

"Who?" Frances stopped in midquestion. I could only be referring to one person. "Come this way."

Dina followed. Peppi stayed rooted to her seat.

Frances took one look at the kitchen and said a couple of words under her breath. She checked Magda's pulse. "She's dead." Then her professional self took over—no longer Frances Waller, high school acquaintance, but Officer Waller of the Grace Gulch Police Department.

She called the dispatcher and gave one of those numeric codes that let other police understand the nature of the emergency. "We need the chief on this one."

The EMTs arrived and went about their business while Frances spoke with us.

"What did you touch?" Frances whipped out her notebook.

"The front door. It was unlocked and there was a note—" Dina began.

"I saw it."

"Magda was expecting us," I said.

"Oh?" Frances started to pursue the subject, but returned to her original line of questioning. "Did you touch anything else?"

"We waited in the drawing room for a few minutes, but when she didn't come, we checked out the rest of the house." I explained how we had checked each room, calling out Magda's name, until we arrived in the kitchen.

Frances made notes and waited with us for the chief. Peppi asked if she could go to the restroom.

Frances hesitated and then hedged. "No. We don't want to disturb anything more than you already have. You'll have to wait." She must have noticed Peppi crossing and uncrossing her legs because she suggested an alternative. "Why don't you go to Cici's store? We'll meet you there."

Peppi jumped to her feet, ready to scoot like a cottontail at the first sign of trouble.

"Don't leave the store after you arrive. The chief will have my hide if you're not there when he comes to question you."

"I'll make sure they stay put," I promised.

"Don't tell anyone what happened." Frances seemed

to think I needed a detailed instruction list.

Of course I won't. Then I remembered our plans for the evening, and I paused at the doorway. "Audie is expecting all of us at rehearsal before long."

"Gene will be there, too," Dina added. "Has anyone spoken to him yet?"

Frances debated for a few seconds. "We'll inform the family."

Including Cord? My heart jerked. Magda's death would echo across every corner of Grace Gulch.

"You'll have to let Audie know you won't be there, but tell him as little as possible, okay?" She made a shooing motion with her hands. "Now go, before the chief gets here."

We drove to the store, opened the door, and rolled down the blinds to discourage visitors. Tonight I didn't need any curiosity seekers.

I called and left a vague message on Audie's voice mail. Dina, Peppi, and I had been held up at Magda's and none of us would make it to rehearsal. Not even Reiner could find fault with that.

"I'm hungry." Dina jumped out of her chair and poked her head in the tiny refrigerator I kept in my office. "You don't have anything in here."

I checked the cookie box—one remained. No one spoke while I divided it three ways, with as much ritual as castaways on a desert island sharing their single meal of the day.

"I can't believe it. Magda—dead! Who would want to kill that sweet old lady?" Pink hair drooping, Dina sounded like she had lost a favorite aunt. Most of Grace Gulch would respond the same way.

"I didn't know her all that long, but she was always nice to me." Peppi sounded a bit forlorn. Magda had that effect on people.

I thought of the threatening e-mail Magda had received and the scene with Gene. It must have some connection to her death, but I didn't want to discuss it with the girls. They didn't know about that particular blackmail note, and I wanted to keep it that way. I would discuss it with Audie—once he had been informed of Magda's death and the police had finished with us.

"What's going to happen to the play now?" Peppi voiced her concern about her first production with the theater. "Magda was the star. And poor Gene. And Cord. And the mayor—no one will want to continue."

"The show must go on." The words came out before I could stop myself.

Peppi burst into tears.

"Cici!" Dina's voice was half scold, half laughter. She patted Peppi's back and handed her tissues. "I can't stop thinking about those pearls. They were Magda's, after all. Someone must have taken them from the theater this afternoon, stole them from props since the last time I checked. I can't believe it's happened again." Last fall, the gun that had killed Penn Hardy had been taken from the theater. "I should have kept them with me until tonight."

Peppi kept crying, well down the road to hysteria. Dina blamed herself for not taking better care of the pearls. I wanted to leave, but we couldn't. We could be stuck there for hours. The police wouldn't get around to interviewing us until after they finished with the crime scene.

I refused to spend the night rehashing the sad events.

16

From: Elsie Holland (Snoozeulose@ggcc.com)
Date: Saturday, April 19, 9:35 PM
To: Dina Wilde (DWilde_GGHerald @ggcoc.net)
Subject: Newsworthy?

 You will interview Magda Grace Mallory soon about an old news story.

 While she talks to you about what happened forty years ago, ask her about what happened eighteen years ago, as well.

 Expect further communication from me on this subject.

Saturday, April 26

*B*ut *what else could we do?* I had promised Frances that we would wait.

First things first. Since everyone was hungry, I called for pizza delivery. Next we needed something to distract us from the horrible sights we had all witnessed; and I knew something that might work.

"While we're waiting, you might as well help me set up my new window display."

I didn't give them a choice; they might decline. I waltzed over to an old-fashioned turntable with an automatic record changer where I played vinyl records of period music. Using a real record player instead of CDs made it seem authentic, another "vintage" item to go along with the clothing.

I rifled through a stack of recordings and chose six to start with, tunes that always set my toes tapping and put a smile on my face. Big band music and swing dance should cheer us up, songs like "In the Mood" and "Chattanooga Choo-choo."

"You're doing the '40s!" Dina caught the drift of my plans.

"You think?" I pointed to the outfit I had laid out to wear on the following day. "Meet Senior Cadet Nurse Cecilia Wilde from the Public Health Service, circa 1943. I'll be showing uniforms of the many branches of the military where women served."

"Our grandmother's uniform." Dina touched the summer uniform with reverence. "I would have liked to have served. Although I might have preferred the WACS." Dina held the appropriate dress uniform against her body and studied her image in the mirror.

"Nah. That olive green clashes with your coloring. Maybe you could be a WAFT." Peppi held up a dress blue which did look good with Dina's fair skin. Not that the Air Force would allow its women to have punk pink hair, even today.

My plan was succeeding. Peppi calmed down a bit. I decided on a little fun. "Now that army uniform would look well on you. Try it on."

"Oh, may I?"

I laughed and waved both of them into the changing rooms. My reasons were not entirely altruistic; pictures of the young women in uniform would make excellent advertising for the store.

I spent a few minutes in front of the mirror, taming my hair into a bun appropriate for a serious nurse cadet in the PHS. Lots of hairpins later, it stayed more or less in place. I took the uniform into my office and changed.

The Andrews Sisters were belting out "Boogie Woogie Bugle Boy" when we all returned to the showroom.

"Hey, I took swing dance lessons. I can show you how to do the jitterbug." Dina, dark blue cap settled on top of her slicked-back pink hair, moved her sneakered feet to the intoxicating rhythm. Well it was too much to expect her to wear matching pumps.

"Whoa, slow down. Show us one step at a time."

The pizza arrived, and between food, music, and dance, we laughed as hard as lonely soldier boys did at USOs far from home, as scared and uncertain as we felt after our discovery. It's a good thing the stores around us had closed; during business hours, they might have complained about the noise.

Peppi took to the jitterbug like a natural. She and Dina decided to try a flip; her arms looked strong enough to hold Dina's weight. Maybe her workout sessions at the gym made a difference. They didn't quite make it. Dina landed on her bottom and slid across the floor, stopping feet away from the door. The doorbell rang. Laughing, Dina stood up, brushed off the dust, and unlocked the door to greet Chief Reiner and Frances.

Reiner touched his Teddy Roosevelt mustache and looked my sister up and down. Then he glanced at me. "So we meet again. After another murder." Somehow the way he said it made me feel guilty by association. The happy mood I had worked so hard to create vanished with the crack of his voice.

"Would you like something to drink, Chief?" I asked. My hair had escaped the hairpins after the second twirl in the jitterbug, and I knew I looked a mess, but proprieties are proprieties, after all.

He ignored the niceties. "I need to speak with you. Now. Peppi, come this way." He led her into my office.

While we waited, my mind wandered. What would have happened if I had been alone when I discovered Magda's body? They say that the person who reports the crime is often the suspect. I was glad I went with Dina and Peppi. Even Reiner couldn't think the three of us were in it together, though he might suspect that one of us had killed Magda and returned with a group in order to deflect suspicion.

I considered that possibility. I didn't suspect Dina, even if I had included her in my steno pad; but what about Peppi? She was an unknown, and that was exactly why I didn't suspect her. She hadn't lived in Grace Gulch long enough to have a reason to murder anyone. But she might be related to that cantankerous Mrs. Lambert in the nursing home. I couldn't discount her as a possible suspect.

Reiner asked about my movements earlier in the day.

I gulped. "I was here." Before he could voice his follow-up question, I added my answer. "Alone." Unlike most weekdays, no one could verify my whereabouts for the afternoon. The store remained closed.

"And what were you doing at Mrs. Mallory's home this evening?"

Straight to the heart of the matter. *Should we tell the*

police about Suzanne, or not?

"She invited Dina and Peppi over for an interview. I tagged along for moral support." We must have created a crime scene expert's nightmare, with all of our footprints and fingerprints overlaying anything the murderer might have touched.

"What was the interview to be about?"

The police had to know about Magda's illegitimate child. And the blackmail threat. I knew several things that the reporters did not. I had already delayed too long in telling the police. "Dina and Peppi don't know the whole story about Magda."

"And you do?" The corner of Reiner's mustache twitched, as if in disbelief.

"Not the whole story, of course not, but I do know something most people don't." I explained about finding the blackmail notes at the theater, though Audie had already given them that evidence. "We were concerned for Magda, so we went to visit her after rehearsal last night." After one final deep breath, I finished with the revelation that Suzanne was Magda's illegitimate child, and Magda's decision to give an interview to Dina and Peppi. Reiner asked me a few more questions and warned me not to tell anyone else.

The office door opened and Audie rushed in. "What's happening?"

Reiner looked him up and down. "Where were you this afternoon between, say, one and two?"

"At the theater." The question didn't ruffle Audie, the picture of innocence.

Reiner grunted and muttered something about no one to confirm his presence. "We'll be back in touch if more questions arise." He touched his mustache in a good-bye gesture and left, Frances trailing behind, the two of them in whispered conversation. Perhaps she enjoyed the hunt as much as I did.

That left the four of us in the store. "Want some pizza?" I popped the remaining slices into the microwave without waiting for Audie's answer.

"Cic!" Audie only shortened my name when he was frustrated. Well I couldn't blame him.

"Cici!" Dina repeated my name. I knew what she wanted to know. *What did you tell the police?*

"Girls." I wanted to redirect their energy. "Don't you need to take the story to the paper?" My eyes challenged Dina. *I can't talk about it.*

"C'mon, Dina. We're in the way now that your sister's shining knight has arrived." Peppi winked at me to let me know she was teasing, and they headed to the changing rooms.

"Eat."

"I'm not hungry." Even so, Audie ate the two slices on autopilot while the girls changed out of the vintage uniforms in record time and left us, at last, alone.

Audie swallowed the last bite of pizza and downed a can of Coke. He wiped his mouth clean. "What happened to Magda?"

"Who said anything about Magda?"

Did Reiner's prohibition against talking about what happened apply to Audie? I decided that it didn't. Audie already knew a lot of it, and the chief had already asked for my fiancé's alibi.

"C'mon, Cic. You know Grace Gulch. The news has reached the farthest corners of Lincoln County by now."

Audie stuffed the empty pizza box into a trash can. "You went there. I want to know the details."

"She's. . .oh, Audie. She's dead. Murdered." The tears that I had held at bay ever since I saw Magda's body spilled out.

Audie took me into his arms and rocked me. Oh, how I loved the man, his strong arms and tender heart. Bit by bit, I gave him the details of our grisly discovery. We comforted each other, arms locked in silent grief, memories of a special woman flowing over and around us.

"Am I interrupting something?" Dina had entered the store without us noticing.

Startled, we drew apart. I confess I was irritated.

"You didn't expect me to stay away, did you?" Dina already had her steno pad in hand. "Peppi had to get to work at the library. What was Magda going to talk to us about? C'mon, Cic, give."

Audie and I carried on a silent conversation with our eyes. I felt like an old, married woman. Out loud he said, "She wanted to let people know. We're not betraying a confidence."

"But—" I considered the chief's warning and decided it didn't apply. Magda intended to tell Dina and Peppi the truth. "Magda had an illegitimate child when she went to Chicago all those years ago."

"I already know that much." Dina shook her pencil at me. "The question is, *who*? Is it someone in Grace Gulch? Does that give that person a motive for murder?"

"It's Suzanne Jay."

That silenced Dina for about fifteen seconds, and then the barrage of questions began. Did Suzanne know? Yes. Who was the father? We didn't know. Did Gene know?

Yes. He just found out. The one detail I kept back was the threatening e-mail. I felt like that was police business.

Dina repeated my description of what we had seen at Magda's house, about the awful blue face, the pearls scattered on the floor.

He drew in a sharp breath. "The pearls? *Magda's* pearls?"

"That makes it even worse. I'm pretty sure they were her pearls. I recognized the clasp. . ." I stopped, unwilling to go on.

"That means—"

"It was someone from the theater. Again."

I thought about my notes about suspects in Spencer's murder and considered showing it to Audie and Dina. *No.* My conscience pricked me. Dina and Audie didn't need to know they appeared on the list.

"I'll have to call the cast and tell them that rehearsals have been suspended until—until. . . ." His voice faltered. How could this production get over murder in the midst? And what would happen to Audie's position with the theater?

"It will all work out. Everything works together for good and all that."

Audie gave me a quick hug. We locked up the store at nine, earlier than we usually left the theater after a rehearsal, but I felt as tired as a bronco after breaking.

In spite of the exhaustion, I had work to do.

From: Elsie Holland (Snoozeulose@ggcc.com)
Date: Friday, April 25, 9:50 PM
To: Lauren Packer (LPacker@ggcoc.net)
Subject: Above the law?

News about Magda Grace Mallory's trust
funds has spread about town. You have acted
nervous about the recent changes to the disposition
of her fortune. Are you concerned for your client—
or for yourself?

I have information that suggests you know
more about the balance in Magda's bankbook than
you're telling.

Saturday, April 26

I knew I wouldn't get to sleep until I considered the
same questions I had raised about Spencer's death with
Magda's. I dug out my steno pad and flipped to the first
page.

*Audie. No alibi—he was alone at the theater all
afternoon.*

He worked for Magda and was in the middle of a
contract negotiation that might provide a motive. But he
was cleared in Spencer's murder, at least unofficially; and I
didn't believe for a second that he killed Magda.

Magda's name jumped off the second page. Elimination as a suspect by death—I slashed through the notes I had made and flipped the page before tears fell again.

Suzanne. Alibi—check.

She and Magda had recently found each other; did she harbor resentment over being given up for adoption?

Lauren. Alibi—check.

He was Magda's attorney. Had she discovered some mishandling of her affairs? Did he resent the increased responsibility she had recently offered Audie?

Mayor Ron. Alibi: probably at the city office.

He was Magda's brother, and they always seemed to be on good terms. So—motive, unknown.

Cord. Alibi—check.

Magda was his aunt. He resented taking Gene under his wing. Angry enough to kill? I couldn't imagine it.

Gene. Alibi—check.

Suzanne's arrival on the scene threatened his position as the heir to the Grace-Mallory fortune, as well as his status as a beloved only child. I could understand if he wanted to kill his newfound sister. But—Magda? It didn't make sense.

Dina. Alibi—at the paper.

She was about to get an exclusive interview with Magda. Why kill the golden goose that would prove her worth as a reporter?

Peppi. Alibi—on assignment from the paper.

She would receive partial credit for the interview. She hardly knew Magda. Motive, unknown. That old lady at the nursing home sure seemed to have a grudge. I needed to find out if they were related.

Frances. Alibi—at work at the police station.

I couldn't think of a motive, unless Magda opposed her relationship with Cord for some reason. It seemed unlikely.

I looked at the suspects. Who was a likely murderer? If I had to pick, I would pin the murders on Lauren. He didn't bother to endear himself to anyone and even seemed to resent Audie's friendship with Magda. Still, she had trusted him to handle her affairs. Personal preferences did not a conviction make.

Sunday church services were a subdued affair. Two murders a week apart did that to a small community. Most people knew Vic Spencer by sight, but we all mourned the passing of Magda Grace Mallory, even our Gaynor-oriented congregation. Pastor Waldberg preached an effective sermon about the uncertainty of life and the two roads we could choose. He sounded better than usual; or maybe we listened more closely in light of the two deaths.

We spent a quiet Sunday, focused on God and family, not murder, although we did read Dina's articles about the tragic events. Monday morning I considered wearing my grandmother's PHS uniform but decided against it. Instead I went with a button-down blouse and wide-legged trousers that women started to wear during the war years.

As soon as I walked into Gaynor Goodies, the barrage started.

"Cici! Have you heard the latest about Magda's murder?" Jessie asked while she assembled two dozen mixed muffins I planned to serve my customers in celebration of reopening the store. Today she wore a blue pin-striped uniform with a frilly white lace apron.

That was a surprise. I had expected questions about the crime scene. "No."

My one-word answer didn't stop the flow of Jessie's conversation. "Her will makes interesting reading. *Very* interesting."

My heart jumped. Dina had written about Magda's new will in Sunday's paper.

"She left money for the theater. . .well, that's old news." *If you considered something that happened a week ago old news.*

"And to that Suzanne Jay person. Your sister wrote quite a story."

Jessie ended the statement with a question mark in her voice, but I didn't rise to the bait. Instead I pulled out a couple of bills and plunked them into her outstretched hand.

Undeterred, Jessie continued. "She left some money for Gene, of course. Not the whole fortune. And she said that she wished she could bequeath her son a strong work ethic instead of money but that is something he would have to learn for himself!" She mimicked Magda's patrician tones perfectly.

I couldn't help myself. I laughed and then felt guilty about it. It wasn't funny for Gene to have his mother's assessment of him broadcast across Lincoln County. If anything, it would make him mad.

Mad enough to murder? The question continued to bother me. I decided to ask Cord if he could verify Gene's whereabouts yesterday afternoon. He might tell me things he would not reveal to the police.

I would have suspected Jessie of the usual Gaynor prejudice against the Grace family if I didn't know that she carried on like this about every story around town.

"I understand that you were there when Dina discovered the body." Jessie held my change in her hand, smiling brightly, as though she might give me an additional discount in exchange for further gory details.

"Yes. I have nothing to add to what she wrote for the *Herald*." I accepted the change and made my escape.

The phone in the store rang while I was pouring water into the coffeemaker.

"How are you this morning?" Audie's low, melodious voice smoothed the feelings ruffled by my stop at Gaynor gossip central.

"Jessie told me the terms of Magda's will. But we already knew that, after Dina's article."

"Ah. Did you escape unscathed?"

I laughed. "More or less. I had already read Dina's article."

"Speaking of Magda's will." Audie paused. "Lauren has invited me to his office this evening to learn the terms of the trust fund. I thought you would want to come with me. I confess, Magda's death has me rattled. How can we continue with the play? And is her offer for a lifetime contract still valid now that she's dead?"

He sounded so discouraged. "Of course I'll come with you. Lauren's office. What time?" I couldn't imagine what he could do to resurrect the play. He hadn't appointed an understudy for the role of Abby Brewster. But we didn't need to figure it out today. "Don't worry about it. I'm sure everything will be all right."

"Is six okay?"

"Sure. I love you."

"I love you more."

"I love you most." We continued in that vein while the coffee finished brewing. After hanging up the phone, I poured myself a cup and opened the box of muffins. One advantage of owning the store was first pick. One disadvantage was the temptation to go for second and third picks. I went for the raspberry orange muffin. It should blend flavors with the raspberry mocha coffee.

So Lauren Packer wanted to see us tonight. Maybe I could slip in a few questions about the murders. Or maybe he would bring up the subject.

The front doorbell rang, and my first customers arrived. Traffic remained busy throughout the day. People wanted to see the spot where Spencer had died. If they were disappointed by the remodeled store, they didn't say so. Others grilled me about discovering Magda's body, and a few even mentioned the pearls. I might as well have spilled the whole story to Jessie. Instead she would hear a garbled secondhand version.

I answered their questions with a minimum of words and turned their attention to the '40s clothing that hung on special racks. Big band music buoyed my mood and a few customers hummed along. By the time I closed up shop, record sales had filled my cash drawer. I would have to make a bank deposit and pick up extra change. Apparently, murder was good for business.

At five minutes to six, Audie walked through the back door, a bouquet of yellow daffodils in his hands. "I thought you could use some cheering up."

"Oh, sweetheart." I kissed him and placed the flowers in a green glass vase that I kept by the cash register. "They're beautiful! Thanks." I looked at the depleted clothing racks and sighed. "I'll have to come back and restock the showroom after we meet with Lauren. Let's go learn what the vulture has to say."

We walked to Lauren's office, down the block and across the street, the second floor of an office building situated next to the old courthouse. The elevator seemed at least a hundred years old when we rode in the creaking shaft. At least the air-conditioning worked. That was nice. The door to Lauren's office stood ajar, and the lawyer himself strode out of his inner sanctum, hands extended, and a smile baring too-straight teeth.

I could imagine his great-grandfather walking out of the same office a hundred years ago, with the same pointed chin and bright teeth, fingers resting on his suspenders. Until the recent mess, I had looked forward to dressing Lauren for his role of Mortimer Brewster in *Arsenic and Old Lace*. Now such everyday pleasures had dimmed, especially with the future of the play in jeopardy.

"Audie, Cici! Thank you for coming. Very pleased to see you both, I'm sure. Come in, come in."

Photographs of Oklahoma birds, including the state bird, a scissor-tailed flycatcher, adorned the walls, and examples of taxidermy flanked the law books on his shelves. A bevy of birds flew around a birdfeeder outside his window. I felt like I had wandered into an aviary instead of into a lawyer's office.

I sat in one of the chairs facing his desk, a deep peacock blue. Audie sat next to me. We clasped hands and waited for Lauren to speak.

"I'm sure you want to know how Mrs. Mallory settled things before her, hmm, untimely demise." Lauren sat behind the desk and put on reading glasses. His chin bobbed up and down while he sorted through the papers in a plain manila folder. He extracted a few pages and slid them to Audie. "Here is a copy of the trust fund Magda created for the arts complex. Information regarding the theater is included in Section Two."

"So plans for the arts center are going forward?"

"Absolutely."

Audie and I bent over the papers, our knees touching, our hands holding the document by opposite edges. We read through it, nodding for permission before turning a page. Through the screen window I recognized the call of a siskin.

Under Section Two, Paragraph C, Item 2, I saw the words "Audwin Howe shall be director of the Magda Grace Mallory Theater for as long as it is his desire to remain so. The terms of his employment shall be. . ."

My sigh trilled in a squeak, as if echoing the birds outside the window. Audie didn't make a sound but his hand squeezed mine. We read the generous arrangements that Magda had made.

Lauren beamed at us. "Mrs. Mallory was very pleased with the job you are doing with the theater, Audie. She hoped that you would settle in Grace Gulch."

Audie lifted my hand and kissed my knuckles. "I have found the greatest treasure of my life in this town."

"Good, good."

Audie's gaze dropped back to the papers. "Who is the theater's new owner?"

Did it matter? Magda had guaranteed his job.

Lauren hemmed and hawed. "We must notify the beneficiaries."

"Of course," Audie murmured.

What few secrets hadn't been revealed by Dina's article.

"—but I can tell you that Mrs. Mallory arranged for decisions regarding the art center, including the theater, to rest with a board, not with an individual."

"Who are the board members? Gene, I suppose. What about you?" Audie lifted his eyebrows at the lawyer.

Or Suzanne? I struggled to keep silent.

"Well, yes, as her lawyer, I will be involved. The director of the complex will be an ex officio board member, as well."

The complex director? That person would be Audie's boss.

"Until the city hires the director, I will oversee the theater as executor of Mrs. Mallory's estate." He curled the papers in his hands like talons. "We must meet soon to discuss the current production."

Did Lauren want to exert control over the theater already? Audie's grip on my hand tightened. His face gave away nothing, however—an actor's control.

The papers confirmed what we already guessed, and held no major surprises. Lauren might interfere for the next few months, but that shouldn't present problems. *Unless, of course, Lauren was the murderer.*

A black shadow crossed in front of the window, a crow landing on the bird feeder. I wanted to ask Lauren about his history with Vic Spencer but couldn't think of a way to broach the subject.

The crow cawed loudly and flapped his wings. The other birds fled. Lauren arose from his chair and shooed the blackbird away, then shut the window.

"I hate crows." Lauren wiped his hands on a white linen handkerchief tucked into his jacket pocket. "That's the third time he's shown up this week. He drives the other birds away."

Ah-hah! He had given me an opening to probe for an alibi.

"People say crows are an omen of death." I didn't believe it, but it sounded good. "I don't suppose you saw a crow on either of the last two Saturdays, did you? That would be too strange."

"Perhaps." Lauren remained standing. "I'm sorry I didn't offer you any refreshment when you came in." He didn't offer any now, either. Maybe he had treated Magda, his client and a person of importance in Grace Gulch, with more courtesy. But he acted as though Audie were a lackey to be summoned and then dismissed.

I plunged ahead. "I just wondered because Vic Spencer died on Saturday. And then of course, Magda died a week later. Two violent deaths a week apart."

"If I were you, Audie, I might stay away from this lady." Lauren's voice remained neutral as he addressed me. "After all, you saw both of the bodies, Cici."

I clamped my hand over Audie's to keep him from jumping up.

I won't let him get to me. I refuse. "And they were both connected with the theater. That's what's so strange. You'd think we were putting on *Hamlet*."

"*Macbeth*," Audie said. "*Macbeth's* considered bad luck."

"Whatever. I'm wondering about other connections that we don't know about. You recommended Spencer to Magda. Where did you meet him?" There, I had asked the important question. I hoped that he wouldn't sue me for slander.

"Some of my clients mentioned that they used his services." Lauren came around the desk. "I can't blame you for wanting to play detective again, after the way you nailed Penn Hardy's killer last fall." He winked at me. "The police might think that you had a motive for killing Mrs. Mallory, Audie, after they learn the terms of her will. Where were *you* on Saturday afternoon?"

18

From: Jerry Burton (cbtrotter@redbud.net)
Date: Monday, April 28, 9:36 PM
To: Peppi Lambert (PLambert@ggcc.net)
Subject: Malice?

You have expressed animosity regarding the special favors that the Grace family receives in the town of Grace Gulch.

Did your animosity extend to Magda Grace Mallory individually?

Expect further communication from me on the subject.

Monday, April 28

*O*f all the. . .
    The lawyer's slanderous question made my chest tighten.

Audie restrained me from lunging at Lauren. He answered in a calm voice, "Why, I was at the theater. Where I usually am in the afternoons." He shook hands with the lawyer and left with all the civility of an afternoon tea party—a better reaction than my desire to draw pistols and call on seconds.

A fixed smile remained on Audie's face until we had

returned to my store. "'Questions are never indiscreet, answers sometimes are.' My brave Cici." He brushed my lips with his and then grew serious. "Lauren's not the only one wondering about me, you know."

He walked into the dressing room, ready to help set the store to rights for the morning. What a man. I brought out several items from my back room. He reappeared a few minutes later, all the articles of clothing hung to show to best advantage and placed on the correct racks. He knew my merchandise almost as well as I did.

"The problem is, no one can vouch for my presence at the theater on Saturday afternoon." Audie talked from behind the skirt rack. "Sometimes Dina is there in the afternoons, but not Saturday. Both she and Peppi had assignments from the newspaper."

"The two of them are thick as thieves recently, that's for sure. They egg each other on like they're in a competition. I'm not sure which one of them is worse." All in all, I was proud of my sister's work at the newspaper, and I liked her new friend. Still, why couldn't they have been on assignment some other day?

I shook out the wrinkles of the dress harder than I needed to with my hand. "Lauren is right about one thing. I do want to find the killer, assuming the same person murdered both Spencer and Magda. It seems like it has to be. Why else would the pearls be used both times?" Tears I had suppressed over Magda's death welled up. "Poor Magda. She only wanted everyone to enjoy her beautiful pearls." The tears came hard and fast. "How could anyone do that to her?"

Audie removed the dress from my hands, and his strong arms encircled me. I looked at the fine blond hairs on his forearm, below the point where he had rolled up his shirt sleeves. Soft-spoken and gentle on the outside, hard and strong in his inner core, where it mattered, that was my guy. I looked into his tearstained, lake-blue eyes.

"Magda was irreplaceable. We have to find out who did this to her." His voice resonated, a bow drawn across cello strings.

"To figure that out. . ." I stopped long enough to blow my nose. "We need to find out who killed Spencer. It's been a week, and the police don't appear to have a clue who killed him. Now that Magda's dead, his case will go cold. But he's the key, I'm sure he is."

"Let's eat before we make any more plans."

I was too upset to cook, so we grabbed some barbecue and headed to the empty theater. If we went anywhere in public everyone would ask about the murders. I couldn't handle that, not tonight. The theater offered a refuge. Also, I needed to recheck the references Spencer provided on his application.

After platters of beef brisket and buckets of tea—at least, that's what it felt like, although we only ate one sandwich each and shared a basket of fries—we examined the list.

Audie glanced at his watch. "It's half-past seven. Early enough to make a visit."

We headed to the first address on the list, one block down the street from my house. The modest ranch house belonged to Dr. Johnson and his wife, my family doctor and eighth grade English teacher, respectively.

"Mrs. Johnson had us read *The Picture of Dorian Gray*. She'll appreciate your Oscar Wilde fascination."

We arrived at the house at twenty minutes to eight

and rang the doorbell. A woman with a friendly face and a blond braid hanging over her shoulder appeared at the door. "Why, if it isn't Cecilia Wilde!" Jean Johnson hadn't changed much since I spent a year in her classroom. "Come in."

I made introductions. She had seen Audie and attended every single play but had never met him personally.

"'Memory. . .is the diary that we all carry about with us.' Cici has told me how much she enjoyed your class."

"I love that quote. *The Importance of Being Earnest.*"

Mrs. Johnson led us into a room full of well-preserved '80s country charm and poured us tea. Neither one of us would get much sleep that night, with all that caffeine, but we wanted to put our hostess at ease.

"Now tell me, what has brought you to my house? I'm sure you didn't come here to discuss Oscar Wilde."

I fiddled with my purse, which held my list of suspects and Spencer's references. My former teacher was too polite to pump me for information about Magda's murder. I would have to bring up the subject myself.

"Mrs. Johnson—"

"Don't be silly. It's Jean. You're not a teenager anymore."

"Jean." Using her first name didn't seem right. In her presence I traveled back in time to the shy teenager I had been. "You probably know that a burglar was found murdered in my store a little more than a week ago."

"I read about that in the paper. You poor dear."

"Did you know the victim—Vic Spencer? The man who ran the cleaning service?"

"Of course. He cleaned our house all last year. A lovely present from my husband for our thirtieth anniversary." Jean's smile relaxed into wrinkled concern, appropriate to the death of someone known to her. "How terrible that he should be killed." She paused, too polite to voice her question. *Why are you here?*

"He listed you as a reference. We thought you might know something about him that we didn't know. We'd like to, er, offer our sympathy to his family." That wasn't really a lie. I had a card ready to send.

"I'm afraid I can't help you. You see, Jack hired him." She moved across the floor with the same decisive strides I remembered from middle school. "Jack. Could you come up here, please?"

A few moments later Dr. Johnson emerged from the basement. No amount of urging could convince me to call the doctor who had removed my appendix by his first name. A light layer of sawdust coated his clothes.

"I can't get away from my tools," he said. "Scalpels by day, saws by night." He noted our presence, not strangers, but not close friends, either, at eight o'clock at night. "Say, what brings you to our neck of the woods?"

"They're here about Vic Spencer."

"The man who was murdered." Comprehension dawned on his face. "At your store." He turned on a professional demeanor. "How are you doing? I understand you also found Magda's body. That's two big shocks."

"I'm fine." As good as could be expected under the circumstances, but I hadn't come to his house for a medical consultation.

"They wondered what we knew about Mr. Spencer. I suppose they feel a sense of responsibility since it happened at Cecilia's store."

Dr. Johnson nodded. This couple understood responsibility. "That lawyer, Lauren Packer, mentioned him when I asked around about cleaning services."

"So Lauren recommended Spencer?" Lauren, again; his name kept popping up.

"Yes, he did. Is that what you wanted to know?"

"Do you know anything about Spencer's family?"

The doctor shook his head. "He kept to himself and did his job. I told Jean we should continue his services."

"And I told him not to be foolish. Why waste money that we could save for our grandchildren's education?" She pointed to photographs displayed above an upright piano. "There they are."

Audie fidgeted as she listed their names. "They're very handsome." He pointed at a dark spot behind the framed pictures. "Did something else used to hang here?"

"Why, yes. We had a small Remington."

Remington, the famous Western painter? His art fetched high prices. My fingers tingled at the possibilities. "That must be lovely. Have you moved it?"

The couple exchanged looks. "Someone stole it, I'm afraid. About six months ago. Together with a few other of our more precious finds over the years." Regret stayed on Jean's face for a moment.

"How awful!" I would check the *Herald* archives on the computer to see if the string of burglaries included the Johnsons. "Do the police have any leads?"

"No." Jean sighed. "I have taken to going to garage sales. I find the most wonderful things, for a fraction of the price."

"I love what you've done with the living room. It's charming."

By the time we left their house, it was too late to continue the hunt.

"We'll have to wait until tomorrow to call the others." Audie sensed my urgency. He shared it, in fact. "I can phone. I can't spend all my time finding a replacement for Magda." A wistful note entered his voice.

"It will all work out. It has to." I agreed to his suggestion. If I called from the store, a customer might overhear and spread the gossip across town.

We arranged to go over the investigation in addition to plans for the play at the theater on Tuesday night. "We might as well kill two birds with one stone." My unfortunate choice of words struck me, and I winced. Audie grinned.

"It's a plan. I'll ask Dina to join us. Ask her to compile a list of the robbery victims."

I must have gaped at him.

"We might as well." He kissed my mouth closed. "If we don't invite her, she'll barge in uninvited. Making it official takes away half her fun."

The following day, I dressed in an outfit reminiscent of Lauren Bacall in *The Big Sleep*. If only my hair were as sleek and lovely as Bacall's, I might even feel like a femme fatale. Instead, I tucked it into a loose bun and added a hat with a black veil over my forehead. That would have to do. The day sped by. I finished the window displays with an enlarged picture of a letter my grandfather wrote to my grandmother during the war. I read aloud one of my favorite lines, "Be sure to keep Old Glory in our window. I'll be home soon."

After I closed the doors and changed the sign to

CLOSED, I thought longingly of a home-cooked meal including all four food groups. Instead, leftover barbecue would have to do. I picked up a ready-made salad from the store and headed to the theater. One of these days, I would cook again. After we nabbed the murderer.

I wasn't the only one thinking of fruits and vegetables. Dina brought pineapple, and Audie added carrots and celery. He rustled up cheddar cheese from the fridge, and we had a feast.

Before we began our discussions, we heard someone walking around the theater. I stifled a groan. Had Dina invited someone, like Peppi, to join us? I didn't really want to make it a foursome.

"We're in here!" Dina's voice rang out. I wanted to kick my sister under the table.

"There you are!" Peppi's red head poked around the corner of the door, and she came in. "I wondered if you had decided anything about the play yet."

"Actually, I—"

"That's not why we're here." Dina cut Audie off in mid-sentence. "Come on in. We're having a council of war."

"About the murders!" Peppi didn't wait for a second invitation. She moved a stack of scripts off a chair and pulled it close to the desk. "I have to show you something."

Audie threw a look my way, shrugged, and handed Peppi an empty plate. "Ooh! Fresh fruit and veggies!" She served herself a healthy portion.

I looked at the two cub reporters. "Before we start, you both have to promise that our theories won't appear in tomorrow's paper."

"Without proof we can't report anything." Dina

grinned, the bright spots dotting her cheeks the same color as her hair. "Brainstorming isn't news."

"Not a hint." Audie said it this time. His deep masculine voice carried more authority than mine.

"Scout's honor."

I checked to make sure Dina wasn't crossing her fingers behind her back. She wasn't.

Peppi nodded vigorous assent. "I just want to get to the bottom of this. I got an e-mail from that Jerry Burton fellow today. I confess I'm a little scared."

Jerry Burton, not Elsie Holland. "Did he threaten you?"

"Not exactly. 'Expect further communication.'" She made quotation marks with her fingers. "But I don't like it."

Audie cleared his throat. "None of us do. I spent the morning checking into Spencer's clients." He opened his date book and ran down a list of names. "Altogether, I spoke with about a dozen people. And they all said the same thing."

19

From: Jerry Burton (cbtrotter@redbud.net)
Date: Monday, April 28, 9:33 PM
To: Cord Grace (cgrace.Circle_G@ggcoc.net)
Subject: Alibi?

   The police will be asking you about the whereabouts of your cousin Gene Mallory on the night of his mother's murder.

   Before you're tempted to lie, consider what happened to Magda Grace Mallory in the safety of her own home.

   Expect further communication from me on the subject.

Tuesday, April 29

What'd they say?" Dina asked the obvious question.

    "They all 'lost' some valuables during the time Spencer worked for them."

    "Those names sound familiar." Dina dug out her steno pad. "I compiled a list from the newspaper articles, like you asked me to. The Johnsons were robbed, well, we already knew that. We also reported about robberies at the Dentons, the Foxes. . . ." She ran down a page of names.

    Dina's list duplicated Audie's.

"So we can assume that Spencer was a thief!" Peppi opened wide her forest-green eyes. At that moment she looked as young and eager as Dina. "Do you think he came into your store to steal something?"

"Magda's pearls." She and Dina spoke at the same time.

"I expect they're worth a lot," Dina said.

My mind flashed involuntarily to the image of the pearls flung around Magda's body.

"There has to be a connection between the two murders!" Unpleasant memories of Magda's body didn't seem to disturb Peppi's enthusiasm.

"It does seem obvious. But what is that connection?" I looked to Audie. "What about the other thing the Johnsons told us? Did everyone agree about that, too?"

Audie grimaced. "I couldn't work it into a couple of the conversations. But yes, most of them have gone to Lauren Packer for legal advice at some time or other."

That tidbit silenced the two girls for about thirty seconds. Dina recovered first. "Lauren? You think he's the connection? Could he be the murderer?"

"He's *a* connection. That doesn't mean he's the murderer." Although the circumstances made him look suspicious. "I do believe he was Spencer's accomplice."

"Several people mentioned they had their valuables appraised at the same time Packer drew up their will. He knew the most expensive pieces in each home, things that they had insured."

"I can see that." Peppi nodded. "Maybe he thought it wasn't really stealing. They'd get their money back."

"How shortsighted. 'No man is rich enough to buy back his past.' You can't buy back memories." Audie studied Dina's list as if the names would change. "We've heard that Packer and Spencer went to college together. That might give us a better idea about their connection."

"I know how to do that." Peppi jumped in. "GGCC has a good interlibrary system with other colleges. I can find out if they went to college together."

"And I'll check the high school." Dina didn't want to be left out of the fun.

"Good ideas. And meanwhile, who else is a possibility?"

"For the. . .murders, do you mean?" Peppi paled slightly. Maybe she realized this was no parlor game.

"We know who benefits from Magda's death, at least what she settled in her will. Gene, of course. Although he won't be getting as much as he expected, with the trust fund and all."

I could have kissed Peppi for avoiding the obvious. As theater director, Audie was connected to both Spencer and Magda; and because of the trust fund, he had a considerable motive.

My relief was premature.

Dina widened her eyes. "Oh, my, they might suspect Audie! We absolutely have to solve the murder!"

A dark red suffused Audie's face, as dark as a birthmark, even darker than a bad sunburn. "I'm more worried about the fact Spencer was murdered in Cici's store."

He's worried about me! His concern touched me deeply. I hastened to reassure him.

"I've thought about that a lot. The murderer has nothing against me. It has something to do with those pearls. . .and the pearls just happened to be at my store."

"That would eliminate Gene as a suspect." Dina bit

into some pineapple, looking thoughtful as she chewed. "He could have taken the pearls at any time before Magda gave them away."

"Unless he wanted to divert suspicion from himself." Peppi speared a cucumber. "Except why would he care about pearls? Why are they so important? Aside from the money?"

"I have no clue." Mrs. Lambert's strange reaction to the necklace raced through my mind again. *Why are you wearing my pearls?* I really needed to go back to see her. I sighed. "I know that Gene is lazy, and I can't say I'm crazy about him, but I never thought of him as a violent person."

"The police are going to suspect Suzanne." Audie's face had returned to its normal color. "I hope I don't sound sexist, but pearls suggest a woman to me. It's the kind of thing a woman might care about. Now that they know Suzanne is one of Magda's beneficiaries—"

Dina continued. "But since she is Magda's daughter—"

"Exactly."

"I think we've done everything we can for tonight." I emphasized the point by closing up the containers of fruit and vegetables and throwing away the empty barbecue box. "Girls, you're checking out the connection between Lauren Packer and Vic Spencer. And Audie, why don't you talk to Suzanne about her inheritance?"

"I already have." This time, pale pink waved across Audie's face. He always had a soft spot for his leading actress. "She says Magda wanted her to start a business in Grace Gulch and settle down. They discussed a loan, but Magda made a permanent bequest in her will 'just in case.' Suzanne had no reason to kill Magda. She wanted her mother, alive and well."

"But the police might not see it that way. I wonder if she has an alibi." I thought about what to do next. "I'll ask Cord about Gene. See if Gene has told him anything or if he knows if he has an alibi for either murder." Not that I knew the exact times of death. First I would check with Frances Waller. She might, just might, tell me the status of the case.

Peppi called me as soon as I opened the store the next morning. The reporter, hot on the trail of a story, couldn't wait any longer. "I've learned something very interesting."

"Oh?" I hoped she wouldn't decide to publish any tidbits she discovered on her own.

"Vic Spencer and Lauren Packer attended law school together! At least until Spencer dropped out. And guess what else?"

I let my silence speak for itself.

"I dug a little deeper to learn why Spencer dropped out. I checked the newspaper morgue and found a short paragraph. He was arrested for burglary just before he left school. He spent some time in prison."

"That clinches our theory, then. He must have been the burglar."

"And Lauren was his accomplice." Peppi sounded gleeful.

"It makes a good working theory. But that doesn't make him a murderer. Did he have a history of violence?"

"Not that I found." The admission pained Peppi.

I made Peppi repeat her promise not to publish any of our research. After we said good-bye, I called Frances.

"Grace Gulch Police Department. Officer Waller speaking."

"Frances, I've learned something that you need to know, if you don't already."

"What is that?" I could picture Frances's brown eyes narrow in interest.

I told her what we had learned about the connection between Vic Spencer and Lauren Packer, what we knew and what we guessed. "And he benefits from Magda's death, too, in a way. She might have learned about his double life. Also, he gets more of a say in what happens at the theater."

"Which brings us back to Audie." I felt Frances's sigh down the telephone wire. "I'm sorry, Cici. We know about the connection between Spencer and Packer, but the chief thinks we have more important fish to fry."

"But—"

"My advice is, don't push it." Frances's voice sharpened. "If he has to focus on someone else, he'll take a closer look at your fiancé."

That silenced me for a few seconds. Surely they wouldn't arrest anyone without definite proof. But they might ignore important evidence while they chased red herrings. And did Reiner consider Audie a serious suspect?

We said good-bye. My insides twisted and turned like a coiled snake. My conversation had done more harm than good. I would wait awhile and give my nerves a chance to settle down before I tackled Cord on the subject of his cousin.

Things had not been the same between us since my engagement to Audie. I guess I should have expected it. Our easy friendship had disappeared, and we hadn't found a new footing. Maybe now that Cord was interested in Frances things would get easier.

Tension or no, I had to speak with Cord to see if I could uncover any secrets about Gene. Secrets abounded in this affair. Magda kept at least one secret hidden, a whopping big one, about the child she gave birth to out of wedlock. Of course that was Suzanne's secret, too, once she tracked down her birth mother. Spencer led a double life, janitor and robber, all rolled into one. That applied to Lauren Packer, as well, respectable lawyer by day and secret burglar's accomplice by night.

Someone—how many? Who?—appeared to know all the secrets and sent threatening e-mails. Had the threats provoked murder?

Even Audie had a secret. A secret surprise that he refused to tell me about.

Audie has a secret. For the first time, the truth struck me. Did Audie's secret give the blackmailer power over him? A cold wind blew across my heart. No, it couldn't. I refused to believe it could. Audie said he had a *good* surprise. And no blackmailer would care about a good secret, would he? Would she?

A steady flow of traffic kept me from calling Cord until lunchtime. I grabbed a container of carrot and celery sticks with a small bucket of ranch dressing and dialed the familiar number.

"Hello?" Cord sounded like he was speaking from the bottom of the river, carried there by the weight of the world.

Shame on you, I scolded myself. Magda was his aunt. Why hadn't I called before now, to offer my condolences?

"It's Cici." I paused to swallow a last bite of carrot and close the lid. "I'm so sorry about Magda."

"I still can't believe it. And poor Gene. . ."

The questions I needed to ask Cord about his cousin stuck in my throat. How could I intrude on their grief? Still, it had to be done.

"How is Gene doing?" In spite of their recent disagreement, Magda had still been his mother—in fact, his only surviving parent.

I knew what that was like, since my own mother had died when I was in junior high. Dad was a rock, a given in a world of uncertainty, as constant as the land he ranched. Now Gene had lost that anchor.

"He's pretty broken up. I know he argued with Aunt Magda, but he was sure it was a temporary problem. He thought she'd change her mind. And lately he's been trying harder at the ranch, at least until he broke his finger working out at the gym."

"Was he working on Saturday afternoon?" There, I'd asked the question.

"What, when Magda died?" No flies on Cord's back. He knew exactly why I asked. "As a matter of fact, yes. I sent him in to town to pick up some supplies at the feed store. He went straight there and back. I can promise you that."

The Mallory mansion was only a block off the straightest route from the Circle G to the feed store. Gene could have strangled his mother and still returned to the ranch on time. I shuddered. Did I really think Gene capable of matricide?

Cord had continued talking. "—feel sorry for Gene. The cousin who had it all. Good looks, money, good education." Cord's parents had died in a car crash during his senior year of college. After graduation he took over the ranch operation without missing a beat. "And now look at him. I'll help him any way I can. We're family."

In those words, I heard the pain and determination that must have marked Bob Grace, our town founder, back when he decided to make the 1891 land run. Did I want to battle the power of the Grace family to investigate any connection between Gene and his mother's murder?

We said good-bye. I stuck out my chin. Last year I had taken on one of the Gaynors, the Grace's rivals in our small world, while investigating the death of Penn Hardy. I would not back down from the Graces, either. No one would complain if Audie and I paid a condolence visit to the grief-stricken son, would they? I decided to stop by after prayer meeting.

Prayer meeting. I hoped the second premarital counseling session didn't reveal any problems with the compatibility questionnaire.

At 5:30 sharp, Audie and I met in the church office. We held hands, Audie's slender fingers trembling where they touched mine, showing he shared my anxiety. The pastor placed our questionnaires side by side and studied them for a long minute.

At last he drew his thick eyebrows together and looked at us.

"Your scores are most revealing."

20

From: Elsie Holland (Snoozeulose@ggcc.com)
Date: Tuesday, April 29, 9:36 PM
To: Reverend Waldberg (word_of_truth@ggcoc.net)
Subject: Secrets?

As pastor of Word of Truth Fellowship, you
are in a position to know confidential information
about suspects in Magda Grace Mallory's murder.

Are you hiding behind clergy privilege?

Expect further communication on the
subject.

Wednesday, April 30

O ur compatibility scores were *revealing*? What did
they reveal? I twisted the cap off a bottle of water
and took a swig. Maybe the drink would moisten my
throat and enable me to speak.

Audie's fingers drummed a fast tattoo where our hands
remained clasped. "I don't care what the score says. I know
I love Cici, and she's the one for me. As Wilde says, 'Keep
love in your heart. A life without it is like a sunless garden
when the flowers are dead.'"

"Now, don't fret." Pastor Waldberg reassured us. His
eyebrows still sent a silent message: *stormy weather ahead.*

"The test works this way: I divide each of your scores by the maximum possible points, then multiply them by a hundred for your individual 'Marriage Compatibility Percentage.' This particular assessment tool says that couples with scores below 50 percent should seriously reconsider the step of marriage—"

Call off the wedding? His words panicked me.

"—and couples with scores between 50 and 70 percent—" He barreled ahead without explanation. "—will need strong conflict resolution skills. Those relationships will require extra TLC."

"What was our score?" Audie asked the important question.

Now Waldberg looked at us, his somber gray eyes saying what his words did not. "Cici scored right at 70 percent. Audie's was a little higher." He shuffled through the papers. "You agree on the most important things; for instance, your spiritual beliefs—your common faith in our Savior, humor, conversation—things that remain as your bodies change and grow older."

I relaxed a bit. Wasn't that most important?

What's the problem, then? My mouth formed the words, but no sound came out. Audie stepped in. "Where do we differ?"

"Well, your scores on the question about your parents varied widely."

"I admire the way Mr. Wilde raised his girls alone. He's a great role model," Audie answered confidently.

I remembered my own score on that question: a five. I rushed to explain. "I've only met Audie's parents once. I like them fine, but I don't know them. How could I answer a question like that?"

"Mm-hmm." The pastor pointed to another question. "This one gives me greater pause. 'I feel that I can share all my feelings, good and bad, with my partner and that he/she does the same with me.' Cici, you only gave four points for that statement."

Now his eyebrows did relax, and I felt like he would listen to my answer. Audie's fingers had drifted to the ends of my fingertips, barely holding on.

"I feel that I do share all my feelings and thoughts with Audie." We worked well as a team when it came to investigating crime, at least.

"So the problem is with me. You feel like I'm holding out on you." Audie turned to the pastor. "I think I understand. You see, I am working on something and—"

I refused to let him skate by. "You keep saying you have a secret and assuring me it's a good one. But if you're planning something for our future, I have a right to know." Anger I had held at bay erupted, and I cried in frustration.

My ever-sensitive and kind fiancé—I had given him a nine in those categories—handed me a tissue. I glared at him.

The pastor looked at me, then Audie. "Are you ready to talk about this tonight?"

Audie shook his head, a slight movement that didn't ruffle his hair.

"Very well, then. I strongly suggest you each spend time in prayer this week. Consider Paul's words in 1 Corinthians 4. 'Therefore judge nothing before the appointed time; wait till the Lord comes. He will bring to light what is hidden in darkness and will expose the motives of men's hearts.' At its heart, this is an issue of trust. Audie, can you trust Cici with your secret? Cici, do you trust Audie's motives? You need to resolve this before we continue with the next lesson."

I thought about that. I did trust Audie's love, and his motive, even if mistaken, could rise out of a desire to protect me. I couldn't discern Audie's thoughts, and I wasn't sure I wanted to.

The pastor led us in prayer and dismissed us to the church dinner. The friendly chatter and quiet minutes spent in prayer calmed my spirit. We would talk, but I could wait until Audie was ready.

A little more than an hour later we exited the prayer meeting to a gray sky, the color that betokens a rainstorm. I would have preferred a moonless night; the threatening clouds reinforced my concerns from the counseling session.

"It's going to rain." Audie had lived in Oklahoma long enough to recognize our weather patterns. "Maybe God is crying for Magda, too. Although I know the angels in heaven are rejoicing." Audie took my hand in his, a simple, comfortable gesture, a reassurance that all would be well between us, and opened the car door for me. We had agreed to visit Gene together.

Audie looked extra nice tonight in a suit that showed off his lean frame to good advantage. But then I thought that about almost everything he wore. Today's outfit suggested a touch of the professor, with the leather-patched elbows and a green turtleneck sweater that brought out the warmth in his blue eyes. I leaned over and kissed him on the cheek. He clasped my hand and held it to the spot where my lips had touched him. At times like this I felt we were as comfortable as an old, married couple, warm and cherished. I was confident that we would work through the issues the questionnaire had raised.

Less than ten minutes later, we parked in front of the mansion. The cloudy sky shrouded the house with an appearance of mourning, as if Magda's death had sucked all warmth and vitality from what had once been a home. A single light burned in the front room, the same room where Magda had entertained us.

"It looks like Gene is home." Audie opened the door for me before grabbing the plate of brownies that I had bought from Gaynor Goodies. At the front door, I saw the clip where Magda's note had hung on the night we discovered her body, and I swallowed past the lump in my throat. I didn't want to fall apart in front of Gene. Sympathetic, yes, but not a basket case, that was the ticket. *Lord, lead me to the truth and let me be a help, not a hindrance, in this time of need.*

Audie was about to ring the bell a second time when it opened a crack.

Unshaven, bleary-eyed, wearing a dressing gown, Gene took a moment to register our identities. "Audie. Cici. Come on in." Bobo recognized us as old friends and danced around our feet.

We followed Gene to the drawing room. My heart sank at the damage done to Magda's home in a matter of days. The same cut glass tumblers sat on the same silver tray, but instead of iced tea and lemonade, I smelled alcohol. At least he used an ashtray to collect his cigarette butts.

Anger burned through me, followed by sympathy. I hadn't ever seen him this bad.

"I'll take the brownies back to the kitchen." I left

Audie with the grief-stricken son.

Audie's low voice rumbled behind me as I made my way down the hall. I paused at the kitchen door, immobilized by memories of my last visit. But I made myself walk through. The police had finished their investigation of the scene and someone else—I was sure it wasn't Gene—had cleaned up.

As long as I was in the kitchen, I nosed around. Magda didn't keep spirits in the house; she had been as dry as the Sahara in her habits. Had Gene slipped back into his old patterns from high school? Rumors suggested that he loaded up after every football game, win or lose. He had straightened out since then; he took risks with money but not drugs or alcohol.

I found a trash can under the sink and breathed a sigh of relief. No beer cans. The whiskey in the front room was probably all he had had to drink today. He could still stop again before he fell back into heavy drinking. Unless he had problems I didn't know about and Elsie Holland/Jerry Burton targeted him?

"Didya get lost back here?"

I jumped at the sound of Gene's voice. He slurred his words and waved around the whiskey glass.

"Here, let me help you with that." I took the glass from his hand and rinsed it in the sink. "Do you want a brownie?"

"Sure." He flopped into one of the straight back wooden chairs that adorned the kitchen table. Bobo lay across his feet. I checked the refrigerator for drinks and poured him a tall glass of milk after I sniffed it. I added a double brownie portion.

Audie appeared at the doorway. "Mind if I join you?"

"Take a chair. Enjoy some of Cici's fine cookin'." Gene tipped over a chair in the process of pulling it out for Audie.

I cut the remaining brownies and put them on the table. Gene demolished half his brownie in a single bite. I offered him another piece.

"Sure is good of you to stop by. It's been lonely around here." Tears welled in Gene's eyes. I felt bad for him. Even after my mother's death, I had never been alone. There was always Dad and Dina.

"I'm sure your uncle and Cord will help all they can." I knew how inadequate that sounded. The mayor and the rancher both had other responsibilities. They couldn't babysit Gene through his grief 24/7.

"Maybe I'll call on Suzanne. The sister I never knew." Gene made a sound halfway between a hiccup and a giggle. "She's the closest family I have left."

I hoped he meant it. Suzanne must be grieving, too. Or did he think he could con her into giving him more of Magda's money?

Gene polished off the milk. I filled up the glass again. I didn't know what to do to help Gene get sober, but I figured milk couldn't hurt. Didn't they say coffee helped? I stood up and poked around in the cabinets. A single red can hid at the very back, behind the many varieties of decaf that Magda enjoyed. I measured out enough for a strong brew, this side of palatable.

While I rummaged through the shelves, Audie and Gene spoke in low voices. The words "Suzanne" and "family" and "relationship" kept coming up. Maybe Audie could communicate better to Gene than I could, man to man.

When the coffee was done, I poured Gene a cup and placed a pitcher of cream on the table. He had trouble getting his fingers around the dainty handle. Two of the middle fingers in his right hand were splinted together.

"You've hurt yourself!" I remembered Cord's mention of Gene's broken finger. Had he injured his hand before Magda's death? In that case, I didn't see how he could have strangled her.

"Oh, this." He cupped the drink in his left hand and carried it to his mouth. His face puckered, and he added a teaspoon of sugar. "I hurt myself working out at the gym last week." His face brightened, as if he had remembered his happy thought. "You know who else was there? Peppi Lambert. Did you know that little firecracker can bench press a hundred pounds?"

"No, I didn't." Although now that he mentioned it, I remembered Peppi's gym schedule. I had pegged her as the intellectual, artistic type, not a health nut. "She's a woman of many talents. She and Dina have been working some newspaper stories together." No need to mention their investigation.

"I won't be making it to any rehearsals for a while. That stupid play. Those unlucky pearls." Genuine tears filled Gene's eyes, and Bobo pressed against his leg. "I asked Mom why she was giving them away. I didn't know she had already made plans to give away half her fortune." A scowl replaced his tears.

The pearls. I had to ask. "Did she tell you why she wanted to—" I almost said "get rid of" but decided that sounded too harsh. "—donate them?"

"Oh, some lame story that they weren't rightfully hers, but the original owner didn't want them back. Hey, you're friendly with that cousin of mine." Gene jumped to a different subject, and his mouth twisted in another scowl. "I won't be going back to work on the ranch. Tell him for me, would you?" He gestured around the kitchen and toward the back door. "I'm a man of business now."

Audie poured himself a cup of coffee before I could warn him about its strength. "From what I know of Cord, he'd rather hear directly from you."

"Oh, yes, my nose-to-the-grindstone cousin, the apple of Mama's eye. Why couldn't I be more like Cord? I've heard it all my life, ever since we were kids." Anger rushed across his face, tightening his features. "And that's hard when your kid cousin is five years younger than you are."

I poured Gene another cup of coffee. I wanted to keep him talking. "I know all Magda wanted was for you to be at peace. She loved you."

"Then why did she leave the will the way she did? Don't deny that you've heard all the dirty details. I tell you, I only get a pittance of the money that's rightfully mine." He grabbed the knife I used to cut the brownies and pitched it into the sink.

21

From: Jerry Burton (cbtrotter@redbud.net)
Date: Tuesday, April 29, 9:38 PM
To: Eugene Mallory (GMallory.Circle_G@ggcoc.net)
Subject: Fingers?

The last few days you have been wearing a splint on your right hand.

Did you hurt your fingers at the gym as you claim—or in tightening the string of pearls around your mother's throat?

Expect further communication from me on the subject.

Wednesday, April 30

We froze for a moment. Audie spoke next. "You'd best be careful. You could have hurt someone."

"So you think so, too. Are you Jerry Burton? Who do you think you are, trying to blackmail me?"

Blackmail? Gene must have received an e-mail from Jerry Burton, and he thought Audie had sent it?

Gene's face crumpled, on the verge of tears. "I would never hurt Mom. She's always been after me, ever since I was a kid, but I loved her. And she loved me. I think she was trying to make up for Dad dying when I was so young. "

"I would never threaten you. I understand more than you know." Audie sat down next to Gene and bent to where he could look him in the eye. "My dad's job took him away a lot when I was growing up. So my mother had to fill in for both parents a lot of the time." Audie sipped his coffee and then added a bit of cream. "I gave her a rough time."

Audie's pale hair fell over his forehead. "In fact, I was arrested for possession of drugs. Not once, but twice. Mom was ready to hand me over to the authorities and let them throw away the key."

Audie had shared part of this story with me before. I thought back to the compatibility questionnaire. *Do you share the same background?* Well, teenage angst was a universal phenomenon; look at Jenna's pregnancy. They both had matured into responsible adults.

I wasn't so sure about Gene. Had he ever been arrested back in high school? Jenna would know. I suspected she held a tender spot in her heart for the Grace bad boy. If so, nothing major had resulted from it. A juicy story about a bad boy from a good family would only swell the Grace family legend. An unpleasant thought struck me. Magda's e-mail mentioned an old secret. Could it involve Gene? Of course not. Gene wasn't even born forty years ago.

"Instead, Mom hooked me up with a Christian lawyer." Audie continued his story. "He told it to me straight. Keep going the way you're headed and you'll end up in jail. Or—go to God. Let Him turn your life around. He can give you what you want from your father." Audie tapped his long fingers on the table, a short drumbeat. "That lawyer introduced me to the theater, and things started to change. If I hadn't paid attention when God

brought him into my life, I don't know where I'd be today."
A smile lit his face. "Certainly not here in Grace Gulch,
Oklahoma, with the woman of my dreams."

Gene sneered. "I suppose you want me to get saved.
Just like my dear sister."

My thoughts flew to the day Suzanne had asked Jesus
into her life after her lover's death threw her world into a
tailspin. Nothing would have pleased Magda more than
for both her children to come to know the Lord.

"I pray that you do." Audie spoke in soft tones that
carried his deepest sincerity. "Every day."

Audie prayed for everyone involved with the theater,
one of the things I admired about him. Gene didn't react,
and we left a few minutes later.

"Do you think he'll listen?" I asked as we drove away.

Audie shrugged. "That's between Gene and God. All
I can do is share the good news with him."

Before I went to bed, I browsed through my closet
for tomorrow's outfit. Even the rationing the war imposed
couldn't stifle creativity. I picked out a white blouse
trimmed with lace, which started life as a pillowcase, and a
denim skirt converted from men's overalls. While I ironed
the blouse, I considered Magda's other heir—Suzanne.
Tomorrow, I decided, I would visit her. She had called
today, canceling our usual Wednesday Bible study.

In the morning, I considered baking homemade
brownies but nixed the idea. Instead, I carried the leftover
fruit and veggies from our meal the other night. Suzanne
watched her weight and might not welcome baked goods.
After work, I drove to Suzanne's apartment, in the same
complex where Frances Waller lived.

When Suzanne opened the door to her apartment,

she looked even more distraught than Gene had, if that was possible. Her normally buoyant blond hair sagged to a dull crown around her head, and she hadn't bothered with makeup. I had never seen the pure, unadulterated Suzanne before.

"Oh, Cici." She choked on my name. "I'm so glad you came by." Old tears had dried on her face, leaving it looking like a squeezed-out lemon.

"I brought you something." I handed her the container of fruit.

"Make yourself comfortable while I freshen up." She disappeared down the hall. I heard noises from the back of the apartment and the flush of water nearby.

Whereas Gene grieved by indulging all his sensual pleasures, Suzanne seemed to have dried up. A pillow and afghan tossed on the couch suggested she had spent the night in front of the television, which played at a low volume. I perused the pictures of Suzanne in her movie roles that hung on one wall. She claimed she had an insignificant career with minor parts, but the photographs indicated otherwise. I righted a frame that had fallen facedown on the end table. Magda had her arm around Suzanne, the two of them smiling into the camera. I recognized it as a publicity shot for the new production.

Suzanne reappeared a few minutes later, her face freshly scrubbed and lipstick adding color to her pale skin. She handed me a mug of coffee. "I'll be back with bowls for the fruit." She saw the photograph in my hand. "It's the only picture I have of Magda."

"It's lovely."

"Peppi was taking pictures of the cast members, and I asked if I could have a copy." Tears gathered in her eyes, and she grabbed for the tissue box. "I promised myself that I wouldn't cry." She tugged the last tissue out of the box. "Where did I put the other box of—"

"Oh, Suzanne." I put my arms around her. It felt as natural as hugging a child with a wounded knee. "I'm so sorry."

My friend relaxed and hugged me back, then let me go. "Let's eat some of that delicious fruit you brought, shall we?" She disappeared into the kitchen and returned with bowls, forks, and napkins. We sat on her sofa.

"Are you looking into Magda's death?" Suzanne eyed me over her steaming coffee.

"Surely, the police—"

"Don't be coy with me. I remember how you went after Penn's killer last year. Please tell me you're on the trail of Magda's murderer. It would mean a lot to me."

"I do think that her death must be connected to Vic Spencer's. You know, the janitor who was murdered at my store?"

"Why?" Suzanne answered her own question. "Because of the pearls?"

"That and other things. And as usual, Reiner seems to be focusing on the wrong people."

"Like me, I suppose." Suzanne laughed at my expression. "Of course I'm a suspect. I'm the unexpected daughter who shows up in time to get a share of the fortune. The chief has been around."

"I don't suppose you have. . .an alibi? For the time of the murder?"

Suzanne laughed out loud. "I wish I did. I was down in Oklahoma City looking at kitchen supplies. I gave them my credit card receipt. I hope that clears me." Laughter turned to a frown. "I forgot the tissues."

I dug a packet from my purse and handed them to her.

She sniffed and dabbed at her eyes. "Something has, rather *had*, been bothering Magda recently. She knew gossip about our relationship would catch up with us eventually, and she wanted to make a preemptive strike. But I don't think that was it."

So something else had been on Magda's mind. Did Elsie/Jerry know about it? "Do you have any idea what it was?"

"Not really. She mentioned paying for past sins. I asked her about it, but she said not to worry, it had nothing to do with me." Suzanne shrugged. "I bet the blackmailer knows. You know, the one who keeps sending those e-mails."

Find the blackmailer, find the murderer. The theme returned, turning logic on its head. It would make more sense for the victim to murder the blackmailer and not the other way around. Wait. Could Magda have been the blackmailer? No. I dismissed the thought as ridiculous.

I stayed with Suzanne for another hour and left before supper became an issue. I wanted to pop into the theater to check on Audie's progress and to put away Magda's costumes.

Audie had left the MGM by the time I arrived. Where had he gone this time? He could have at least left me a note or phone message. I went straight to work on the costumes. Each cast member kept their accessories, scripts, and other personal items in a cubbyhole, but sometimes they left their costumes there, as well.

Audie wanted a '30s feel to the play, and he turned to me for advice. I gave Uncle Teddy a suit coat with patched elbows and designed hand-sewn cotton dresses with wide collars for the Brewster sisters. The neckline on Elaine Harper's dress dropped to a fashionably daring low; Peppi's dress, with the gathered waist and slim hips, emphasized her slender figure. Magda was almost as slender as the twenty-something actress; I added padding to give her a matronly look. Whoever took her place would need a new dress. If someone took her place. If the play was produced as expected.

I blinked back tears as I put the dress that Magda would never use into a garment bag and hung it on the clothing rack. I noticed the clutch purse that Peppi carried in her scenes lying on the floor. Really, she could be careless. Out of habit I picked it up and carried it to her cubbyhole.

When I put the purse away, I saw a glimmer. A single, shining pearl, perfectly oval in shape, fell from the cubby and rolled around on the floor.

I stared at it. *It can't be.* Was it the real thing? For a second I debated the legality of touching the object. *Why not?* I found it in the theater, where no crime had taken place. Any connection with the murders was pure conjecture.

I picked up the shining oval and held it to the light. I recognized the luster, the opaque color, the precisely matched size. I would stake my professional integrity on this being one of the pearls from Magda's necklace— pearls I had last seen scattered around the floor in Magda's kitchen.

How did it get here? Did Peppi pick up one to keep? How? The police had arrived minutes after we made the 911 call and bagged all the pearls as evidence.

I scrambled to think of an explanation for the presence of a pearl in Peppi's cubby and could think of none. Peppi seldom wore jewelry. The hair on my arms stood on end. I didn't like the direction of my thoughts. I could be wrong. Perhaps Peppi had lost a pearl earring. Perhaps someone else had dropped it.

I knew one way to confirm the pearl wasn't from Magda's necklace. I dialed the police station and asked to speak to Officer Waller.

"Yes?" Frances sounded frazzled. Two murders in a single week could do that to a police officer, I supposed.

"I've got a question." If she refused to answer, I didn't know how else to get the information I needed. "How many pearls did you retrieve from Magda's kitchen?"

"Why do you need to know? You won't be getting them back this time, at least not until after the trial."

I didn't want them back. I could never again handle them with pleasure. "It's for insurance purposes." I wasn't exactly lying; I did need to file a claim.

"Okay. Give me a minute." I heard fingers clicking on a keyboard. "Evidence log says we retrieved 29 pearls."

"Okay, thanks." My desire to protect Audie and the theater warred with my conscience. The pearl I held in my hand was solid evidence, not conjecture. "Um, Frances?"

"What else?"

"I found another pearl here at the theater. I'm pretty sure it's from Magda's necklace."

"Are you sure? How do you know?"

"There were thirty pearls on the necklace. I counted them when I had it appraised. And I studied them, you know? It just looks right."

"Where did you find it? Never mind. I'll come right over."

I heard the buzz of the phone in my ear. I didn't have scientific evidence, but I knew it was the missing pearl. But what was it doing in Peppi's cubby? Had it been planted? Or had Peppi left it there?

Start with the obvious. I had raced past Peppi's name as a possible suspect when I listed cast members a few days ago. I dug out the list and studied the notes on her page. I hadn't followed up on any of my questions about her, like whether or not she knew Suzanne or Audie back in Chicago, or whether she was connected to the miserable Mrs. Lambert at the nursing home.

I tapped the end of my pen on my teeth and added more notes and questions. *Pearl belonging to Magda's necklace found in cubbyhole. What is the relationship between Magda, the pearls, and the Lamberts, if any?*

What was it that Mrs. Lambert had said when she saw me wearing Magda's pearls? Something about the pearls belonging to her and her son giving them to a harlot? Even knowing that Magda had given birth to an illegitimate child, I couldn't imagine describing her as a harlot. But maybe someone who knew her in her wild youth might. Who could I ask? The people who knew her best, like the mayor, would never answer a question like that. How could I learn the history of Magda's pearls?

I found a blank page and wrote "pearl found in Peppi's cubicle" at the top of the page. Of course someone else connected to the theater could have planted it there. I flipped back through the previous pages. Unless I wanted to include everyone in Grace Gulch, because we all had some kind of connection to Magda, the same pool of suspects applied. They all had access to the theater.

I went through the familiar names in light of my

discovery. *Audie.* As with the threatening e-mails, he had the best opportunity to plant something in Peppi's cubby. I couldn't imagine any connection between Audie and the pearls; however, the police would.

I ran my fingers over Magda's page and tapped the note at the bottom. "Murdered" was written in dark letters, circled, and underlined.

Suzanne Jay. Did the pearls have any connection with the illicit romance that resulted in her birth?

Lauren Packer. Was he scamming Magda? Locating high-priced goods for Spencer to steal, including the pearls? Did she threaten him? Could he have tried to substitute paste jewelry for the genuine article? I shook my head. If so, he failed. The necklace in my keeping was the real thing.

I wanted to skip the pages for the mayor, Cord, and Gene. Why would they kill her? They were Magda's closest relatives, which put them under the microscope. Okay, perhaps the necklace was related to some family secret; perhaps they didn't like Magda's decision to give away a family heirloom. They might know about the history of the jewelry, some unknown fact that would point to a motive. I thought of Gene's injured finger. Could I learn when he had it set?

As props person for the theater, Dina had handled the pearls. History repeated itself because last fall she had also handled the murder weapon that shot Penn Hardy. In fact, she was the only person, besides me, that I knew had touched them. I swallowed past the lump in my throat. I hoped that the police wouldn't focus on her as a suspect.

Next up were Peppi and the mysterious Mrs. Lambert who accused "that harlot" of taking the pearls. How could

I interrogate a senile old woman? For the life of me, I couldn't think of a single reason why Peppi would want to kill either Vic Spencer or Magda Grace Mallory.

The last name on my list was Frances Waller. I knew of no connection between her and the pearls. I didn't really think the police officer was a murderer.

The only solid clue I had was the pearl in Peppi's cubbyhole, which anyone could have dropped there.

Back to square one.

From: Cici Wilde (Cici's_Vintage_Clothing@ggcoc.net)
Date: Thursday, May 1, 9:17 AM
To: Audwin Howe (AHowe_MGM@ggcoc.net)
Subject: Secrets?

Audie. . .we need to have a serious talk. When I called your cell phone, I got a message that said you were "out of area."

Where do you keep disappearing to? Remember the pastor's words.

Call me tomorrow.

Thursday, May 1

I set my notes aside when Frances arrived but pulled them out again at home. This time I prioritized my suspects.

I discounted most of them. Audie and Suzanne had alibis for one of the murders. Cord had only limited opportunity and no known motive. Dina, Frances? They didn't make sense.

That left Gene and Lauren. They both had strong apparent motives for murdering Magda. I debated about Peppi. I found the pearl in her cubby, but someone could have planted it there. What motive did she have to harm Magda or Spencer? Still, I included her among the strong suspects in the murders. I would focus my questions on those three.

Ideas for pursuing answers played around in my head as I sorted through my closet for what to wear tomorrow. A black-and-white flowered rayon rockabilly dress—perfect. Before I changed into my nightgown, I heard a sharp rap at the door. *Who on earth?*

I opened the door, and Audie immediately gathered me in his arms. "I've missed you." He kissed me as if a week had passed since he had seen me, instead of a single day. "I'm sorry I missed your call."

"I went to the theater tonight," I told him. "I thought you might be there?" I made it into a question.

"I couldn't settle down to work, so I took a drive to clear my head."

I bit my tongue. I didn't want to conduct an argument on my front porch. "Come on in."

"Maybe, for a few minutes."

He followed me into the silent living room. I flicked the radio on low volume, as was my habit.

"Would you like some tea? Coffee?" I headed toward the kitchen, anticipating his answer.

"No, thanks. Can you close your store tomorrow?"

That stopped me in mid-stride. "Close the store? I just reopened. Why?"

"I want to show you something." Audie smiled, but the cloudy blue of his eyes betrayed his uncertainty. "It will only take a few hours. Like you said, we need to talk."

Two different ideas flew into my head at the same time. Was Audie ready to tell me his "good" secret? In that case, I couldn't refuse. Also, I needed time away from the store to continue my investigation.

"Of course. I'll ask Dina to cover for me while I'm gone." This semester she had several online classes and never minded coming in when I needed her. "Can we go in the morning?"

Relief at my answer turned Audie's eyes back to a clear twilight blue, stars sparkling in his eyes. "Yes," he said and he kissed me good night.

I went through my bedtime routine with a happier mood than the last several evenings. I reconsidered the next day's outfit in light of my new plans. Everyone in Grace Gulch knew my penchant for wearing everything from half bustles to polyester, but the rockabilly outfit might look outlandish once we left town. I decided on a black dress, always timeless, even if this one had square shoulders, belted waist, and a military cut that had '40s stamped all over it. Magda's pearls would have been the perfect accessory for this dress. I put my head in my hands and allowed myself a quiet sob over my friend's death. *Oh, Lord, I want to bring her murderer to justice. Help me.*

I awoke earlier than usual and studied my notes. In case the opportunity to ask questions arose today, I wanted to prepare. After a little thought, I logged onto the MGM web site where we had posted publicity photos in happier days. I printed them out and tucked them in my purse.

Audie, dressed in blue jeans and a denim shirt that made his eyes shine, picked me up at my house at eight. His casual attire told me a little about our destination; we weren't headed anywhere stuffy, like an office.

He whistled. "Don't you look good, soldier girl."

I saluted him smartly, and he laughed. "Do you want to stop by Gaynor Goodies before we leave?"

I agreed, and we exchanged banter on the way to the store. I felt more lighthearted than I had in days. The prospect of spending a morning with Audie did that for me. We were laughing as we walked into the bakery.

Jessie, dressed today in a peacock-blue uniform with pinstripe apron, raised an eyebrow when she saw us enter together. "The happy couple. I don't often see you together. Busy with wedding plans today?"

I couldn't answer if I wanted to because I didn't know our destination. But that wouldn't stop Jessie from spreading a story about honeymoon plans or some such thing by day's end. I bought cookies to drop off with Dina, and one bran muffin and a large cup of regular coffee for myself. I indulge in the leaded version in the mornings. Audie bought a bagel swimming in cream cheese. After a brief stop by my store, we headed down the turnoff that would take us to Route 66.

"Do you mind if we stop at any pawnshops we run across between here and wherever we're going?" I wouldn't give Audie the satisfaction of asking him for details about our secret destination. I would let him surprise me. I fished the cast photographs out of my purse. "They might have seen Spencer or his accomplice selling the stolen items."

"Can't get you away from your murder inquiries, can I?" Audie grumbled, but he smiled. "Have at it, my dear Miss Marple." He glanced at me, and his eyes lit with pleasure. "Although looking like that, perhaps I should call you Mrs. North."

"Why, Mr. North, we're not even married yet." Secretly I was pleased.

Ahead of us, a trio of neon signs flashed on and off. Pᴀ ɴ ʜᴏᴘ—the same stores I had visited last week with Dina and Peppi.

No one recognized anyone in our photographs.

"Don't worry," Audie said. "I'm sure the thief went farther afield. We'll stop at more places along the way. Unless you're in a hurry to get back?"

"Dina can stay as long as I need her today."

We stopped one more time before we hit Route 66, and Audie wandered off the highway a couple of times to locate pawnshops. Again, none of the clerks could identify anyone in the pictures. My hopes flagged.

We hit pay dirt in Arcadia, at a pawnshop within sight of the red roof of the town's famous round barn. This particular establishment had some nice jewelry for sale, unlike the other stores, which sold mostly junk.

I showed my pictures to the clerk, a beefy, muscled guy who looked like he would be more comfortable on the back of a bucking bronco than behind a counter. "Do you know if you've dealt with these people any time in the last six months or so? They told me about some earrings I would like to wear at my wedding."

He covered a yawn with the back of his hand. He must hear a dozen hard-luck stories a week. People didn't sell good pieces like the hypothetical earrings I had mentioned for fun. I doubted that he cared about their reasons. He barely glanced at the pictures and shook his head. "Nope."

Audie stepped in. "Bob." He glimpsed the man's left hand where he wore a wedding band, then he looked him in the eye with all his actor's sincere ability. "You're married, aren't you?"

"Yessiree!" Bob the bronco buster transformed into a good ole boy. "Me and Missy got hitched at Christmas."

"And you remember how Missy wanted everything perfect for the wedding, don't you?"

Bob's head nodded up and down.

"That's how my fiancée here feels about finding the right earrings. She wants to wear them at the wedding. Something old, you know? Her mind can't rest until she finds them."

It was a version of the truth. I had occupied myself with the hunt for the murderer to the exclusion of everything else, including wedding plans.

"So if you could look at these pictures a little more carefully, we'd appreciate it."

Audie's man-to-man talk did the trick. Bob spread the prints across the counter. "It wasn't either of these women." He put aside Suzanne and Peppi's pictures. "But this guy has been in here a couple of times." He pointed to Lauren Packer's photo. "What was your jewelry like? Maybe I'll remember it."

"Why, thank you," I burbled, as excited as the jittery bride Audie had described. "That's *so* helpful. I remember now." I described those earrings listed among the burgled items.

Bob's face lit up. "I remember those earrings." The smile fled. "But I'm afraid that it's already been sold. I'm so sorry."

"That's disappointing. Maybe Lauren has some of the other items." I made myself sound discouraged and not elated. "I'll ask him as soon as we get home. Maybe it's not too late."

I refrained from skipping until we exited the store.

Then I allowed myself a small hop of joy. "That confirms it."

"Lauren Packer and Vic Spencer were working together in a burglary ring," Audie agreed. "No wonder they had their eyes on Magda's pearls."

Should I tell the police? No, Frances had dismissed that whole connection. My satisfaction lasted as clerks at two more stores along the way confirmed that Lauren Packer had utilized their services. By then I was trying to tie the burglaries in to the murders.

"Do you think Spencer argued with Lauren? And so he killed him?"

"And Magda somehow guessed and so he killed her, too?" Audie considered the possibility. "Lauren must have known about Suzanne. Before all the brouhaha, I mean. When Magda had him change her will."

"Lauren might have blackmailed Magda about a secret she revealed to him herself. That would be an awfully sick thing to do, taking advantage of your client like that. No wonder Shakespeare said, 'First thing we do, let's kill all the lawyers.'"

"I never have liked Lauren. Oh, he knows how to turn on the charm. He plays Mortimer Brewster to perfection. But when he's just being himself. . .I don't know. He feels cold, somehow." Audie drummed the black leather on his steering wheel. "Do you want to stop anywhere else? Or can you put it out of your mind for a few minutes?"

I tilted back my head and let out a long sigh. "I can do that." Bright April sunshine streamed through the windshield, warming my face and teasing the worries out of my heart. A soft breeze wafted through the trees, turning over the leaves on the oak trees, swaying the purple heather like sea grass. It was a perfect spring day, and I was with the man I loved. I shut blackmail and murder out of my mind.

On our way out of Arcadia, we drove past several cafés. Audie pointed to the out-of-state license plates of the cars in the parking lot. "I bet I can guess which people are the tourists." The smug smile on his face made me want to laugh. He had settled into life in Grace Gulch, but as long as he kept those flat Chicago vowels, no one would ever mistake him for an Okie.

Soon city sprawl replaced the backcountry road. Audie was driving to the suburbs around Oklahoma City. The area had been built up since my last visit to the state capital. Several years of nonstop construction had improved the I-35/240 exchange. We passed by the Ford Center, home to the recently relocated OKC Thunder. I doubted that even an NBA team would ever take the place of the Sooners and the Cowboys in the hearts of true Okies, however.

Could Audie understand that kind of passion for college sports, coming as he did from a city that boasted not only one but two major league baseball teams? My thoughts flashed to the compatibility questionnaire, with its question about similar backgrounds. Sports were the least of our differences. Today, maybe, I would learn Audie's secret.

I kept up a running commentary on all the changes. It might seem like small potatoes to my big-city fiancé, but I reveled in the progress. I only hoped that it would never reach Lincoln County. I didn't want big city life to invade Grace Gulch.

When we headed into Moore, I wondered just how far Audie intended to drive today. "We're almost there."

Audie broke his silence. He exited the highway and made a few turns until we reached a quiet corner near the city center. A domed white brick building in need of some repair sat back from the street. The exterior suggested marble archways and cool interiors. A sign stood on the lawn, overgrown grass piercing the broken glass. The words MOORE COMMUNITY CENTER were written in faded black paint.

"We're here." Audie opened the door for me, and we stood at the edge of unkempt grass, looking at the building. He took my hand and led me to the entrance.

"A theater?"

In answer, he took a brass key from his pocket and opened the door. Cool air greeted us. A few dusty, wooden folding chairs dotted the floor in front of a stage, a very intimate setting, room for maybe two hundred seats. Definitely a theater, smaller than the MGM. Why did Audie have a door key?

Streaming sunlight set Audie's hair afire with a deep golden color. He tilted his head as if to absorb the atmosphere of the place. I tried to identify the emotions that played across his features.

Homecoming. He looked like he had at long last returned to the place he belonged.

Scary sensations bubbled up my throat, making it hard for me to speak. "Audie. What's going on?"

From: Jane Marple (knittinglady@redbud.net)
Date: Thursday, May 1, 9:36 PM
To: Cici Wilde (Cici's_Vintage_Clothing@ggcoc.net)
Subject: Magda Grace Mallory's pearls

You found Magda Grace Mallory's body.

If you want to learn more about her pearls,
talk to Lola Lambert.

Friday, May 2

Audie drew a deep breath, as if to compose himself, and took my hands. "A group of churches in the Oklahoma City area just bought this building. They want to start a theater ministry."

One shoe dropped and echoed in my mind. I looked around the empty room, the space begging to be used. "And?"

"They've asked me to be the director."

The second shoe fell, a silent thud. I dug out a tissue from my purse, dusted off a folding chair, and sat down. How could Audie exclude me from this important decision?

"Please say something."

"Something." When Audie didn't smile at my feeble joke, I continued. "How long have they been in communication with you?"

"About a month."

I uncapped the bottle of water I carried in my purse and took a long drink. Maybe it would cool off my increasing anger. What could I say?

"So this was your secret." My voice was as flat as the Oklahoma panhandle.

"Yes." If Audie sensed my hesitation, he didn't respond. Instead he trotted to the farthest corner of the room. "Listen." His excited whisper carried clearly. "The acoustics are perfect. This theater is a gem." He took me on the grand tour, showing me dressing rooms, entrances and exits, and such.

Nothing much registered; my thoughts took a different road. I had guessed that Audie wouldn't stay in Grace Gulch forever, in spite of the provision in Magda's will. But so soon? Before we even married? Tears gathered behind my eyes.

Audie stopped at center stage. "You know I've always felt theater was my calling. I could do a variety of things here. Some community theater, maybe some musicals, definitely biblical dramas."

I felt like the audience on the receiving end of a performance and not his future wife. Why didn't my normally sensitive fiancé pick up on my hesitation?

He grasped my hands between his. "The pay is good, very good. I want to provide for our family. This may be my best chance."

What about Grace Gulch? What about my store? I couldn't meet his eyes. Those deep pools of blue would bore into mine, begging me to dream with him. I felt more than saw his shrug.

"I could commute. It's not that far. I feel like this

theater could really minister to people. I know that Magda guaranteed me a lifetime position with the MGM. But with Lauren as acting director of the Center for the Arts. . ." Audie blew out a breath. "Well, let's just say he's a better actor than a boss. Magda had a knack for management; I don't think Lauren does."

Lauren. I was growing to hate the name. Possible murderer and thief and now husband-stealer.

"Look at me." Audie lifted my chin with his finger. My lack of enthusiasm had doused the fire in his eyes. "I won't accept this job if you don't want me to. I would never do anything to hurt you. I have to agree with Wilde's definition of selfishness. 'Selfishness is not living as one wishes to live; It is asking others to live as one wishes to live.' I want to love you like Christ loved the church."

Oh, Audie. I pressed my lips together to keep from crying. *In that case, why did you wait so long to tell me about this job offer?*

"I realized that Pastor Waldberg was right. I was hogging this offer to myself when I should have trusted you with it. I'm sorry I didn't tell you before. Please forgive me?"

I looked into clear eyes which reflected nothing but love and honor, and I touched my engagement ring. I opened my mouth to say yes, but instead what came out was "How could you?" I began crying in earnest.

"I'm so sorry." He put his arms around me and repeated his apology. "I was wrong. I know that now, and I won't do it again."

He kissed me then, a gentle caress, one that reaffirmed and renewed our commitment. "Just pray about it, will you?"

I smiled at him through a blur of tears and promised

I would. We left a few minutes later. City dwellers might consider the drive back to Grace Gulch a short commute, although nothing could beat the five-minute drive from my house to the store. He dropped me off a few minutes before noon.

Dina, her pink hair almost complementing the '80s punk rocker look she adopted for the store, reported a brisk morning's sales. "I did some research on Marjorie Dresbach, the WASP officer you featured in your window display. Interesting! I'd like to write a feature on her." She waxed eloquent on the subject, her reporter's enthusiasm engaged.

What would my sister do if Audie accepted the other position? Would the new director of the MGM use her services as props manager? I wouldn't stay involved, not without Audie; theater was the lifeblood of our romance. I couldn't spend evening rehearsals with him in Moore. Our dreams seemed headed in different directions, dreams that could tear our lives apart. What had Pastor Waldberg said, that couples with a 70 percent score on the compatibility test would need good conflict resolution skills? I never expected to have his assessment put to the test so soon. I wanted to follow Audie's leading, but what about my hopes and goals? More than anything, why hadn't Audie told me as soon as the offer came up? I stewed about it all afternoon.

Suzanne came into the store about mid-afternoon. Audie's possible change of jobs might also disrupt her life, although I doubted any director would let go of the most experienced performer in Grace Gulch. I was tempted to ask her but couldn't betray his confidence.

"I wanted to thank you for coming by the other day.

Enid has visited, too, but that's been about it."

Bless our pastor's wife for doing what she could in Suzanne's grief.

Suzanne's smile would seem sincere to someone who didn't know her actress's tricks. "I'm trying to think the best of everyone. No one knows quite what to say, you see. Do they mention the fact that Magda was my mother or not? Those are the kind ones. Others can't decide whether to congratulate me on my good fortune or to suspect me of hastening her to an untimely end."

"Have the police given you any more trouble?" Frances had indicated suspicion fell on my friend.

Suzanne shook her head. She examined a cloche like the one Gene Tierney wore in the movie *Laura* and placed it on her head. It suited her. "They're satisfied with my alibi. But that doesn't stop the gossip." She adjusted the angle of the hat. "I'll buy it."

"Magda's gone home." I wrapped the hat in tissue paper before laying it inside a hatbox. "To a better place."

"And best of all, I'll get to see her again." This time Suzanne's smile was genuine. "Magda was so happy when I became a Christian. But I can't help thinking what if. The murderer robbed me of something precious."

"I miss my mother, too." I dreamed of the sage advice she could have shared about my conundrum with Audie. Even if she couldn't advise me, she would have listened.

"That's right. You lost your mother when you were in high school."

Junior high, actually, but I didn't correct her.

Another customer came in, and we couldn't continue our conversation. Suzanne left without our speaking further. During a lull in business, I checked my e-mail.

If you want to learn more about her pearls, talk to Lola Lambert, it read. This e-mail came from Jane Marple, the sleuth in the same mystery that featured Jerry Burton and Elsie Holland. Was it the same person?

But—Magda's *pearls*?

Everyone assumed the motive behind Magda's death lay in the disbursement of her fortune. I wanted to confirm my hunch that another reason stemmed from events buried in the past. I had to get to the nursing home to talk to Mrs. Lambert.

Dina returned about mid-afternoon. "Did I leave my hat here?"

I retrieved her pink embroidered "Girls Rule!" ball cap from the shelf underneath the cash register. She had exchanged the leather vest she wore in the morning for a pink T-shirt. She looked like cotton candy on two legs. "Great! Peppi and I are going bike riding after we study."

Peppi. Maybe Dina knew if her friend was related to Mrs. Lambert. "Do you study at her family's home?" I hoped that the roundabout question would start the ball rolling. A direct question would arouse Dina's investigative instincts.

"She lives here on her own. No family in the area." Dina scrunched up her face. "Wait a minute. She's mentioned a grandmother who lives close by."

"That's nice. It must be lonely, far away from her family. Maybe we should invite her over for Sunday dinner." Mrs. Lambert had to be Peppi's grandmother.

"I'll ask her." Dina sketched a wave and left.

During another lull in the afternoon's business, I called Lauren Packer's office. I thought I could determine his alibi for the time of Magda's murder, if I could catch his part-time secretary. Young Wilma Olmstead was beauty-pageant pretty, if you discounted her habit of chewing gum. Lucky for me, thoughts rattled around in her head like stray marbles. Hopefully, my questions wouldn't arouse any suspicions.

"Lauren Packer, attorney at law." Wilma spoke with the clear, crisp tones of an actress. Audie should recruit her for his next production. If there was a next production. If he was here to direct it.

"Hi, Wilma, this is Cici Wilde. I'm afraid that I've gotten things confused, with everything that's been going on." I paused. Was I lying? Not really. I did intend to make a new will after the wedding.

"Mr. Packer offered to meet me at his office on Saturday afternoon. I know that's a special kindness. I thought the appointment was tomorrow, but when I looked at my date book, I had written down last Saturday, at two. I don't know if I wrote down the wrong date or what."

Lauren often made his own appointments. Wilma wouldn't question me.

I heard Wilma ruffling through paper. "I'm sorry, Cici. I don't see your name listed for either Saturday."

"That's strange." The pretend puzzlement I put into my voice would have impressed Audie. "I could swear he set up a special time for me on Saturday. Does he keep track of his weekend appointments? Maybe he forgot to write it down." I held my breath after I reached the crucial point. I hoped Wilma would cooperate, not question my reason for asking.

I heard the rustle of pages. "No, he didn't have any office appointments last weekend. He marked through both days with a big X, indicating he wouldn't be coming in. He must have forgotten to write it down. I can reschedule. What time is convenient for you?"

"I'm not sure. Please don't bother him about it. I'll call you back when I'm ready." And when I did make my will, I would go to my regular lawyer, Georgia Hafferty.

I felt guilty for misleading Wilma, who was so friendly and helpful. What had I learned, after all? So what if Lauren was out of the office on a Saturday afternoon? No one expected a lawyer to keep weekend hours. Still, it suggested he had opportunity, and we already knew his motive.

I dug out my steno pad and made notes of my conversation with Wilma before the end-of-day rush started. What other leads could I investigate? Did I need an excuse to visit Mrs. Lambert? I didn't think so.

On impulse, I called Enid Waldberg, the pastor's wife, and asked her to go with me to the nursing home. "I need to speak with Mrs. Lambert." I explained the strange e-mail and the questions it raised about Magda's pearls. "She seems to know something. I'd appreciate your company. You might help neutralize the atmosphere."

"Of course." Enid's gentle laughter came down the line. "I'll be happy to be your Watson for the evening." She arrived at the store a few minutes after six, and we drove straight over to the senior facility.

Mrs. Lambert sat in the same green chair as last week, her back ramrod straight, fire sparkling in her dark eyes. She might be unpleasant, but her passion for life stood out among the people who suffered from Alzheimer's or worse. I shuddered.

Enid returned greetings to a few residents, inquiring after grandchildren and bingo tournaments. At last she neared our target.

"Mrs. Lambert. How are you this evening?" Enid used her best pastor's wife voice. She was dressed in confidence-inviting attire, a soft, pink sweater over gray linen slacks. Curling brown hair gone to gray framed her face.

"You're Enid Waldberg. From that Word of Faith Church."

"That's right. And this is my friend, Cici Wilde."

Coal-colored eyes focused on me. "You were here the other day, wearing that harlot's necklace."

From: Jenna Wilde (The_Wilde_West@taos.arts.com)
Date: Thursday, May 1, 4:12 PM
To: Lauren Packer (LPacker@ggcoc.net)
Subject: Monday appointment

Mr. Packer:

*This e-mail confirms our interview at 10 a.m.
on Monday, May 5.*

*I look forward to discussing the opportunity
you mentioned during our phone conversation.*

*Jenna Wilde
The Wilde West Art Gallery
Taos, NM*

Friday, May 2

At least Mrs. Lambert's hostile statement about the
pearls gave me an opening.

"Yes, I wore pearls. It sounds like there's quite a story
behind the necklace."

"That Mallory woman." Mrs. Lambert harrumphed. "Sit
down. I can't talk to you when you're towering over me."

Enid pulled two chairs close.

"Why do you call Mrs. Mallory. . ." I couldn't bring

myself to use the word "harlot." I cleared my throat and restarted. "Why did you dislike Mrs. Mallory?"

Mrs. Lambert settled into serious storytelling mode. "People around here think she was some kind of saint, but I didn't like her when she was alive, and I won't pretend different now that she's dead. My son, Philip, dated that harlot in college. He fancied himself in love with her and heard wedding bells. One Christmas he asked for my pearls to give to her." She responded to the surprised look on my face. "Yep. They belonged to my family. My pa gave them to my ma. Well, the next thing he knew, that woman left Oklahoma for parts unknown. Broke his heart, she did. And now we all know what happened. That harlot went off and had a baby out of wedlock."

Could Suzanne Jay be Mrs. Lambert's grandchild?

She answered my silent question. "Not my boy's baby. He was a godly man, kept himself pure for marriage."

How can she be sure? I kept my suspicions to myself; I tended to believe her. No wonder Magda gave away the pearls. Did she feel guilty every time she looked at the expensive reminder of a serious romance? Did she feel like she accepted them under false pretenses? I wondered if Magda had suspected that Peppi was the daughter of the boyfriend of her youth. If I got the pearls back to sell, I'd make restitution to Dina's friend.

"How pleased you must have been when he found someone else to love," Enid interjected. "God is so good at giving us second chances."

Mrs. Lambert's coal-colored eyes gleamed with pleasure. "That He did. I thanked God the day my Philip married Polly. And then they gave me those two darling grandchildren."

"I believe I know your granddaughter. Peppi?"

"Peppi's such a devoted granddaughter. She even moved back to Grace Gulch to be near me. She visits every week, you know." Recognition blazed in her eyes. "Wait a minute. Are you related to that pink-haired young woman?"

At least "young woman" was polite. "Dina's my sister."

She harrumphed, expressing her opinion of pink hair and probably the world in general.

"Peter doesn't visit often at all. He did invite me to his wedding."

Peter Lambert, Peppi's brother? *Peter, Peter, pumpkin eater.* We used to make fun of his pumpkin orange hair. He went to grade school with me and moved away after that. Peppi wouldn't have started school yet, so I had never met her.

An attendant moved among the residents and approached us. She handed Mrs. Lambert a small pill.

Enid looked at me. *Are you finished?* I nodded.

"We've kept you too long." Enid stood and wished Mrs. Lambert a good evening. I felt those coal eyes burning a hole in my back

When we reached the front door, Mrs. Lambert's scratchy voice rang out, "Come back and see me any time. And bring that pink-haired gal with you."

"She seems to like you." The corners of Enid's lips turned up. "Did you find out everything you needed?"

"That story about the pearls surprised me. No wonder she disliked Magda so much." I climbed into the passenger seat of Enid's van. "But there's no way she crept out of the nursing home and committed murder." It didn't give Peppi a motive either, even if she knew. Why would she care about her father's old girlfriend? Why, that would be like my future child killing off Cord because we once dated. It didn't make sense.

Enid brought me to the parsonage for beef stew, redolent with garlic and a hint of apple juice, tender pearl onions, potatoes, and carrots. Her husband lost his fiery demeanor away from the pulpit. I watched the comfortable banter between husband and wife and ached over the problem with Audie. What if I had to leave Grace Gulch? Friends like Suzanne and Enid were rare jewels. I didn't want to start over again somewhere else. *Lord, give Audie and me unity about Moore. Change my "wanter," if that's Your plan for us.*

Saturday morning I put on my Rosie the Riveter outfit. The coveralls were comfortable until I had to use the restroom. The day spun forward, with too many customers to give me time to pursue my investigation. A good day's business was worth the delay.

When I pulled into my driveway after work, a car with a rental company sticker waited on the street. My front door opened and a tornado dressed in a beaded, fringed jacket tore down the steps. Jenna, my wayfaring older sister, had returned and welcomed me to my own house. We hugged.

"Bet you didn't expect to see me, but I didn't think you'd mind."

I took note of the signs of Jenna's presence. A single backpack hung on my coatrack, probably her only luggage. A faint scent of jasmine lingered in the air, and she had rearranged the pillows on my couch in an asymmetrical pattern. Today's copy of the *Herald* was spread across the coffee table.

"C'mon to the kitchen. I made some coffee."

I chose milk over coffee and cut up an apple. She dug a packet of sweetener out of her jeans pocket and poured it into her cup.

"This is the week we're getting fitted for the bridesmaids' dresses, isn't it?"

Given recent events, I had put off making a decision about the dresses. But I still had a week; the fitting was scheduled for next Saturday. Why was she here a week early? She must have read my mind. "Oh, I know I'm early. I thought we could hang out together? Next thing you know, you'll be an old married lady, and I'll be the old maid aunt."

"Not that soon, I hope." I didn't doubt Jenna's desire for "sister" time, but I was equally sure she had ulterior motives in showing up seven days early. In the past she couldn't wait to get out of our small town.

"Soon enough." She blew on her coffee. "You're the first Wilde girl to settle down and get married. Who'd a thunk it?"

Jenna's words revealed regret she seldom expressed. She gave birth to Dina at fifteen and had wisely given her baby to Mom and Dad to raise. Now I wondered if she left Grace Gulch after high school because it was too painful to stay. She steered clear of further romance.

"There's someone special out there just for you, I'm sure of it." I patted her shoulder. "If God could bring Audie here all the way from Chicago—"

"Enough of that." Jenna shrugged off my attempt at solace. "This is your big day coming up. Tell me about your plans." She wiggled her eyebrows, a trick I envied. "And fill me in on the murders." Amber light glowed in her hazel eyes, so like Dina's. Her zest for life filled my kitchen.

"Where do I start?" I expected "at the beginning" in reply. Wasn't that the standard answer?

Instead she asked, "What's the first thing that pops into your mind when I say 'wedding'?"

"Move." *I didn't really just say that, did I?* Jenna was the last person I wanted to discuss Audie's job offer with. But maybe I was wrong. Maybe she could give me an outsider's perspective.

My answer left her speechless for a moment. "Are you and Audie planning to move after the wedding?"

"No. Yes. I don't know." I told her about the theater in Moore. "We could still live in Grace Gulch, but then he'd have to commute. I would never see him, between my store hours and his evening rehearsals."

Tears spilled out of my eyes. Wedding jitters, grief for Magda, and worry about the thief who invaded my store— my *life*—flowed through me. Jenna put her arms around my shoulders, not saying a word. At long last I stopped crying.

Jenna brought me a cup of spearmint tea, one of the varieties of herbal infusions she introduced me to years ago, and waited while I mopped up my face with a damp washcloth.

"I bet the cry did you good. What a rotten week." She dished out a bowl of ice cream, ultimate comfort from someone who avoided dessert like Texas in July. "But you're getting in a tizzy about unimportant stuff. You love Audie, and he loves you. And that's all that matters."

A wistful look flitted across her face, so fast that I almost missed it. I wondered again if my carefree older sister hid a secret longing for home and family.

"God will show you where He wants you to live."

And as she said it, I believed her. I trusted God, and I trusted Audie. God wouldn't lead us in opposite directions. Whatever the compatibility test hinted about the success of our marriage, whether we lived in Grace Gulch or Moore, or even New York City someday, God would show us the way. "I can't wait." At that moment, I wanted to fast-forward through murder investigations, the play production on hold because of the death of its leading lady, and decisions to be made about the future, to the day of our wedding on a perfect June evening at twilight.

"Promise me you won't elope." Jenna's voice had a lilting, teasing quality. "Dina would never forgive you."

"Neither would Dad. I'm not sure if he's looking forward to marrying off one of his daughters or if he's sorry to see me go." No doubt he would be unhappy if I moved away from Grace Gulch the way Jenna had. I felt the stirrings of empathy for her decision to escape the confines of family expectations at the age of eighteen. I knew she would support us, whichever job Audie accepted.

"Ready to look at wedding dresses now?" She patted a gallon-sized Ziploc bag she had laid on the table.

I laughed. "I've got my own stack." I disappeared into the study and came back with a folder of catalog pages and computer printouts of wedding dresses I liked. That was the problem. I liked so many of them and couldn't decide if I wanted a simple, nostalgic wedding reminiscent of the nineteenth century, an elegant wedding with full skirt and train that would have done Grace Kelly proud, or something more contemporary like an Augusta Jones dress. I advised people all day on what clothes to choose.

Why couldn't I decide for myself?

Jenna sorted my printouts into two piles, one much smaller than the other. I assumed they were "possible" and "definitely not." I studied one of the rejects.

"What's wrong with this one?" I rather liked the contemporary style, strapless, with silver bands adorning the bodice.

"Uh-uh. You would never be comfortable in a strapless dress."

I looked at it again. She was right. It looked good on the model and maybe on me, but it felt too immodest. Another reject looked a bit like something straight out of Jane Austen with a dash of the early twentieth century added in. "What's wrong with this one?"

Jenna looked at me as if I had lost my senses. "It's all wrong for you. You've got a lovely shape—I've always rather envied you that—and you want Audie to see his beautiful bride, not a washboard in white walking down the aisle."

I looked at the pleated front of the dress and laughed at Jenna's washboard description. She did have a point.

"Don't second-guess me." Jenna wagged her finger at me as I ruffled through the rest of the rejects. "You know fashion, but I know what looks good. I deal in art. I can visualize it on you." She paused at the next catalog page. "Oh, my, this is perfect." She looked from me to the picture and back again. "Yes. Definitely."

I couldn't stand the suspense. I snatched the paper from her hand, ready to argue with her opinion. Instead my breath caught in my throat as the perfect dress jumped off the page. Demure and romantic, contemporary yet classic, the dress captured my essence and would show off my best points. I flung my arms around Jenna.

"You're the best big sister a girl could ever have."

From: Elsie Holland (Snoozeulose@ggcc.com)
Date: Friday, May 2, 9:32 PM
To: Eugene Mallory (GMallory.Circle_G@ggcoc.net)
Subject: Jenna Wilde

The eldest Wilde sister has returned to town.
Are you interested in renewing your acquaintance?

Is new romance in the air? Or is it the stench
of an old crime?

Expect further communication from me on the
subject.

Saturday, May 3

After we agreed on the dress, the remaining wedding details fell into place. The rest of the evening flew by while we considered bridesmaid gowns, colors, flowers, the reception, everything. I would discuss relevant details with Audie later, but I knew, on a level where I didn't question it, he would love it.

Close to midnight, when we set aside the plans, I couldn't come down from the clouds. In a reversal of roles, I kept Jenna up, chatting nonstop.

The numbers on my bedside clock passed one o'clock before she complained.

"Aren't we going to church in the morning? I need my beauty sleep, even if you don't."

I stayed locked awake and talked to my heavenly Father. *Thank You for bringing Audie into my life and for whatever You have for us in the future. Thank You for Jenna, and for the way she helped me tonight. Thanks for keeping us safe.* At some point during my phone call to God in the middle of the night, I fell asleep.

Sunday was a somber affair. We shared a short family dinner at the ranch before attending the memorial service for Magda. Even wedding plans couldn't lift our spirits more than a couple of inches from the ground, and by common consent we agreed to meet again later in the week.

A light touch on my shoulder woke me just as my alarm went off on Monday morning. Jenna turned it off. "Sleep a bit longer. I'll take my shower first and start some breakfast."

I wondered if a shape-shifter had taken my sister's place. Maybe she put her best foot forward in happy emergencies like weddings.

When I woke up again forty-five minutes later, I could smell caramel truffle decaf brewing in the kitchen. I followed the aroma down the stairs and poured myself a cup. I expected the ultra-healthy, ultra-crunchy cereal Jenna favored for breakfast, but instead she had boiled eggs and cut up fresh grapefruit. My mouth salivated.

"I'll put on my face while you eat." She rinsed her plate and cup and left.

A few minutes later, the water in my own shower turned cold, shocking me into awareness. Shivering, I hurried into my clothes for the day—a vintage knit jersey from the University of Oklahoma. It didn't look much different than the ones on sale today. The more things changed, the more they stayed the same.

I stopped in the front room and gawked at my sister. My Southwest casual sibling was dressed in her equivalent of formal wear: a denim skirt, button-down blouse, and pretty beaded vest with high heels, even. She had made up her face carefully, as for an important date with a new guy.

"Close your mouth before you catch a fly." Jenna's smile promised mischief and secrets.

"What's going on?"

"It's no big deal. If it works out, you'll be the first to know."

Anyone who knew Jenna could tell it was a big deal. I clenched my jaw. Did everyone have a secret they were keeping from me? I forced myself to relax. After she helped me so much on Saturday, I could forgive her almost anything. I stopped at Gaynor Goodies as usual.

"I'll take a box of cranberry orange scones."

"Jenna's back in town." Jessie used tongs to lift scones into a box. Today she looked like a sour apple lollipop in her green uniform and matching striped apron.

"Yes." I didn't expand, but that didn't stop the town gossip.

"I hear she's in line for that new Visual Arts Center. All those years in Taos finally paid off. I'm sure you'll be glad to have her back in Grace Gulch."

I steeled my face not to give away my surprise. *Jenna, why didn't you tell me?* I felt foolish learning the news this way. How ironic that Jenna might return to Grace Gulch when Audie and I might move away.

Another thought jumped onboard as I walked across

the street to my store. If Lauren Packer hired Jenna to run the Visual Arts Center, did that mean he had decided against making Audie the director for the entire complex? Would he hire someone else? Or had Audie already refused him? Told him he had accepted another position?

Jenna swung by the store mid-morning, accompanied by Dina. They were laughing, their faces matching cartoon cels from the same animator's hand. A silhouette artist would have a hard time differentiating between them. Dina had her mother's forehead, generous mouth, and perky nose. Only her cheeks and chin hinted at her father. Jenna had never identified him, and we never asked.

I poured three cups of coffee. "I guess the interview went well. You got the job at the Visual Arts Center?"

"You knew?"

"Oh, I know everything."

Jenna's face fell like a deflated balloon, and I had to laugh.

"Jessie told me." *Why didn't you?*

"I didn't want to tell you until it was a sure thing. It's still not official until I sign the contract, but Lauren offered me the job this morning! As managing director of the visual arts program at the new Center for the Arts! Audie might be my boss!" She started to say more, but she looked around, taking in changes to the store.

"Oh, I *love* what you've done with it." She touched the photograph of our great-grandparents' homestead. "I remember that cast-iron skillet!" She pointed to other antiques displayed around the store. She slipped on a pair of glasses to look at the letters our grandfather had sent to our grandmother during World War II. "This is so much nicer. More. . .personal."

She opened the door to the bathroom and clucked at me. "Now, this has got to change. I have just the idea."

I didn't know what problem Jenna could find with the bathroom. It was perfectly clean, well stocked, and even big enough to turn around in.

Jenna extracted a small sketch pad from her purse—as constant with her as Dina's steno pads—and drew a picture of a sink with a skirt to hide the ugly water pipes. She then painted a window on the right-hand wall. "If you like it, I can fix it for you." She smiled. "After all, I'll be here for several days."

I looked at it. "It's charming. Thank you."

Jenna made a note of the supplies she would need. "I'm coming back to stay, girls." She opened her arms wide and declaimed in her most Jenna-like voice. "I thought I had to leave to find what I wanted. And for a long time, I was happy in Taos. But I finally realized that all I ever wanted was right here in good old Grace Gulch." She clapped her hands together like a pair of crashing cymbals and hugged the two of us. "My sister and my own dear, grown-up daughter."

Did I see a hint of panic in Dina's hazel eyes?

"And of course all those years in Taos gave me the experience I need for this job, and contacts in the art community. I wouldn't have gotten this job straight out of college."

Should I warn Jenna that her future boss was a murder suspect and almost certainly a thief? I opened my mouth, preparing to jump in. One had to take one's opportunities with Jenna. Once she wound up, she tended to talk nonstop. The phone rang. It was Lauren Packer.

"Cici, I'm glad I caught you. Have you seen Audie today?"

"No. Why?" *Are you going to tell him he didn't get the job as director of the arts complex? Tell him you've hired his future sister-in-law instead?* I guess he hadn't actually decided on the director yet.

"I've been calling his cell phone, but he isn't answering. It says it's out of area."

The theater in Moore is out of the calling area. Surely Audie hadn't decided to accept the job before we talked again.

I heard voices in the background. "My next appointment is here. I've left a message, but have him call me if you see him first." He said good-bye in his most lawyer-like voice. Not that lawyers sounded any different than the rest of us, but his officious tone made his transformation into the suave Mortimer Brewster in the play all the more amazing.

Jenna examined stock she hadn't seen for several months. "Do you have any new hats?" Hats were her passion.

I grinned. "How about this?" The green straw hat with a navy bow whispered "Jenna" the first time I saw it.

"Perfect. I want to look my best—a different best—tonight. And maybe. . .that scarf?" She picked up a chiffon number with swirling colors.

Dina made rabbit's ears behind Jenna's head. "She has a date. With Gene Mallory."

Jenna did unexpected things, but a job interview with one murder suspect and a date with another, who was also a supposedly grieving son, were a bit much, even for her. Of course she didn't know I suspected either one of them of murder.

"That's a speed record, even for you."

Jenna shrugged, tipping her head this way and that

while she looked in the makeup mirror. "He was coming into the lawyer's office after my interview. We started talking, and well, one thing led to another."

"I already told her that Gene is on the A-list." Dina shrugged as if to say, *I couldn't stop her.*

"I can't believe the two of you." Jenna took the hat off and handed it to me to wrap. "You've known Gene all your lives. He's harmless."

"We knew the suspects in Penn Hardy's death, too, but that didn't stop us from investigating. Promise me you'll be careful, okay?"

"I promise."

"The hat's perfect," Dina announced. "With that new cappuccino shade lipstick, you'll look as pretty as the redbud in bloom." They were as bad as two girls dressing for the prom. She did a jig. "Jenna and Gene, sitting in a tree, K-I-S-S-I-N-G. First comes love, then comes—"

Jenna turned a shade of pink as bright as Dina's hair. "That's enough." The laughter that laced her words let Dina off the hook. She paid for the merchandise.

The two of them waltzed out the door, heads bent together in whispered conversation. Surely Jenna couldn't—wouldn't—be seriously interested in Grace Gulch's resident bad boy. But maybe at thirty-four she might be desperate enough to marry the next man who asked her.

It's high time you stop feeling jealous of your sister. She might be prettier than I was, but I owned my own store and enjoyed the love of a wonderful man. Still I couldn't help wishing I had a little of her zest for life. Try telling a clown fish to be satisfied when he shared an aquarium with a goldfish.

Audie appeared about fifteen minutes after my sisters left. I hugged him tight and kissed him.

"Whoa." Audie wiggled in my arms, locked his hands around my neck and kissed me back. "Now, that's better." He smiled. "To what do I owe the honor of that welcome?"

"Jenna came by."

"Ah." Audie understood my ambivalent feelings about the sister I dubbed "Hurricane Jenna." He even shared them.

"Oh, I'm supposed to tell you. Lauren Packer wants to speak with you as soon as you're back in town."

"I got the message and stopped by his office before I got here." His eyes clouded. "We've got to talk about my job situation."

Uh-oh. Here it comes.

He sighed. In another era he would have been twisting the brim of a fedora between his fingers. "I headed back to Moore this morning."

From: Jerry Burton (cbtrotter@redbud.net)
Date: Sunday, May 4, 9:36 PM
To: Elsie Holland (Snoozeulose@ggcc.com)
Subject: Threats

> *I know your identity.*

> *Expect to hear from me soon.*

Monday, May 5

Audie made a decision about the job? Without talking to me about it?

I didn't know which upset me more: the thought of moving to Moore or the fact that Audie made a unilateral decision.

"I couldn't do it." His lips turned in an apologetic smile. "I was going to turn down the job. But then I kept thinking how the pastor said we need to trust each other. I turned the car around. We need to make this decision together, whether we stay or go."

He paused. He expected, wanted, *needed* a response from me.

His statement registered deep in my psyche. "You turned around." I started to sing inside.

He gathered me into his arms. "I'm trying, Cici. I have a lot to learn. There's something else you should know.

Lauren's offered me the position of the executive director of the new arts complex, overseeing all the programs, as well as continuing as director of the theater."

Something inside me relaxed. An old memory stirred, and I had an idea. "Can you come with me in the morning?"

"With you? Anywhere." Audie brushed my hair with his fingers.

"There's a place I've gone in the past. When we found out Jenna was pregnant and the house was in an uproar. Again, after Mom died." I drew in a deep breath and held his hand. "I'd like to go there with you tomorrow morning. I want us to pray before we make a decision."

"Sounds like a good idea." Audie stroked his chin. "Let's ask Pastor Waldberg to pray for us, as well."

We arranged to meet shortly after dawn. Didn't Jesus often pray at that hour? After a brief good-bye kiss, Audie left.

When I arrived home shortly after six, every light in the house blazed. Jenna had exchanged the morning's fringed jacket and denim skirt for a chartreuse silk blouse and pleated navy linen skirt. Her new straw hat perched on her golden hair like a tiara. She would blow Gene away.

"Are you really interested in Gene?"

"What's that?" The words came out garbled as Jenna held bobby pins between her teeth and pinned the hat on her head.

"Gene. Do you really like him?"

"It's more that we're kindred spirits." She pulled the hat off her head and started over. "Bad girl, bad boy. No one quite willing to believe we've grown up."

In Gene's case, at least, I agreed. If he had ever done an honest day's work in his life, he kept it well hidden.

"You don't really think he committed the murder, do you?" Jenna adjusted the tilt of the hat.

I shrugged. "He had opportunity and motive. I think it's either him or Lauren Packer or possibly Peppi Lambert."

"Lambert. That sounds familiar." This time Jenna's attempts to pin on the hat succeeded. The front doorbell rang. "Tell him I'll be there in a minute, will you? I need to freshen up my lipstick."

I peeked out the window at Gene. His face was pale, the probable result of the sorrow of the past few days. Dressed in shirt and tie, he looked more mature. At least he hadn't brought the faithful Bobo along for the date. I went downstairs and let him in.

Jenna took enough time to try five shades of lipstick before she came downstairs.

Gene's eyes lit up when she made her entrance. And a grand entrance it was, dramatic and purposeful.

"I hope I haven't kept you waiting too long."

"No problem." Gene looked willing to wait until the next full moon, if Jenna wanted.

Jenna smiled shyly, pleased by the impression she'd made. Then she turned to me. "Before I forget, I remembered the story that circulated about the Lamberts. They left town about twenty-five years ago, right?"

I nodded. "Peter was in my class until fifth grade, then they were gone until Peppi came back."

"I remember. His father taught freshmen English. He died in some kind of mysterious auto accident. We talked about it for weeks. Then the next thing we knew, the Lamberts had disappeared."

"To Chicago."

A solid thud made us both turn. Gene slumped against the wall. I slid a chair under him before he could fall to the floor. A greenish hue tinged his already pale face.

"The Philip Lambert who taught English was Peppi's father?" Gene croaked out the words.

I fanned his face. "Yes. What's wrong?"

"I need something to drink."

Jenna took the change to their evening's plans in stride and walked into the kitchen. She reappeared a moment later, twisting off the cap of bottled water. Maybe Gene wanted something stronger, but he wouldn't find it in my house.

He took a long swig. He lifted the bottle to look, as if the refraction of the light might return everything to normal. When he spoke, his voice sounded as gritty as gravel.

"I drove the car that killed Philip Lambert."

"What do you mean?" Jenna's voice cut the air. "We all thought it was some out of town hit-and-run driver."

I took the bottle from Gene's shaking hand before he could drop it.

"We let everybody think that. Mom told the police that she was responsible for the accident. Uncle Ron—he was already on the city council, even back then—convinced them to hush it up." Tears ran down his cheeks. "But Mom wasn't driving the car. I was. I shouldn't have been driving; I only had a learner's permit. I had been drinking and, well, I killed a man. I told you I'm no good for you, Jenna."

Jenna stood stock-still, no doubt immobilized by

shock. Then she knelt beside Gene. "I've made my own share of mistakes. God's forgiven me, why won't you let Him forgive you?" She put her arms around him and started praying.

My mind ran along a different track.

Did Peppi know the official version? That Magda Grace Mallory claimed to have killed her father?

Revenge. Now, that was a motive for murder.

Perhaps I should have told the police about Gene's confession, but I wasn't ready to do that yet. They already knew the official version of the accident, which might provide a motive for Peppi to murder Magda.

Audie and I met for our prayer vigil at half-past six. The first molten gold startled the day awake as we drove down the dirt road to the meadow at the back end of the Crazy W Ranch. Dad said that my great-grandfather left the stand of trees alone to please his wife. The romantic notion enchanted me. Breathing in the heady scent of lilacs mixed with pungent cedar made me feel close to heaven. It was my favorite place to go pray, my personal burning bush.

Audie came prepared for our vigil. "Remember how Pastor Waldberg told us we seemed to have an issue with trust? Well, I looked it up in a concordance. I learned so much." He took me on a tour of the word "trust" in his favorite book of the Bible, Proverbs.

"I realized I'd been placing my trust in the wrong things. I wanted the job in Moore because I thought it would bring security. Well, Proverbs 11:28 warns that 'whoever trusts in his riches will fall.' I kept the opportunity to myself, but again in Proverbs we're told, 'He who trusts in himself is a fool.' I've told you that you're my woman of noble character, but unlike the wise King Lemuel, I didn't put my full confidence in you. Worst of all, I didn't really trust God. And until I 'trust the Lord with all my heart,' He can't 'make my paths straight.'"

This was the man I wanted to be my husband and father my children. "Take the job in Moore, if that will make you happy. I don't care about the salary or if we have to move. I'd rather be with you in the center of God's will than miserable on my own."

"Dearest Cici." Audie traced the curves of my face. "Let's ask God what He wants."

As we studied and prayed and talked, God gave us clear direction. I knew we would come here again, the next time a decision loomed.

Hours later, we prepared to leave. "I've called a cast meeting for this evening." Audie lifted my left hand to his lips. "We've got to move forward." His blue eyes glittered like perfect sapphires. It felt so good, so right, to be one in spirit again.

His cell rang. He covered the mouthpiece and whispered. "It's Chief Reiner, returning my call." He lifted his hand and spoke into the phone. "That's right. We're rehearsing tonight. . .I understand you're in the middle of a murder investigation. . .I'd really appreciate it if you could come anyway."

I motioned for Audie to hand me the phone. I didn't feel right withholding the information I had learned. "Chief, did you know Gene Mallory drove the car that killed Peppi Lambert's father?"

Reiner spoke in his no-nonsense, stay-out-of-cop-business tone. "The incident report indicates that Mrs. Mallory was driving at the time."

At least he didn't pretend ignorance. "Gene explained that he did it, but his mother took the blame. The thing is, Peppi may believe Magda killed her father. That sounds like a motive for murder to me. Remember the pearl I found in her cubbyhole at the theater?"

"We are investigating all angles."

I struggled to keep my voice steady. Why was he so obstinate? "Just think. Gene Mallory, Lauren Packer, and Peppi Lambert will all be at the rehearsal tonight. And Suzanne Jay, of course, although I understand you have confirmed her alibi. There might be fireworks when we get them all together." I used my most wheedling tone. "We'd really appreciate your presence, Chief, in case something happens."

"Fool of an idea, if you ask me. What does your fiancé think he's doing, holding a rehearsal with multiple murder suspects in the cast?" Silence lasted for a heartbeat then he blew out his breath. "But I can't stop you. Either Frances or I will come."

I closed the phone and looked at Audie. "Someone will be there." Now that we had made the arrangements, I wondered if we had made a mistake. A shiver at odds with the bright May sunshine passed down my spine.

"This production seems doomed." Audie slapped the steering wheel. "You'd think we were producing *Macbeth*, not *Arsenic and Old Lace*."

"It will come together. You'll see. It's like the postal service—come rain or sleet or snow or sunshine—"

"Murder and burglary and arrests, oh my." Audie

twisted his mouth in a wry smile. "It's a good thing God knows how this will all come together, because I don't have a clue. Well, maybe I do." He pulled a list out of his pocket. "I brainstormed who could take over each of the roles in the play, in case something else happens. Tell me what you think tonight." He bussed my cheek. "I want this to be the best production the MGM has ever put on. Magda's memory deserves that much, at least."

I waved good-bye to Audie as he walked out the front door. Across the street, Jessie closed up shop at Gaynor Goodies. I bet she would add my morning's absence from the store to the rumor mill. I waved at her as if all was right with my world.

To be honest, I did feel a certain euphoria, the thrill of the chase running through my veins like a drug. I stopped by my house to cut up some fruit for the rehearsal and arrived at the theater a few minutes late.

Peppi pulled up next to me. "Can I help you carry anything?"

"Grab the bag of ice, will you?" I kept my voice neutral, willing myself to act as if nothing had changed.

Perhaps I expected a somber mood among the cast, with Magda's death hanging over us like a dark cloud. Instead, an excited buzz greeted my ears as soon as I opened the door.

Dina noticed me struggling with the bowl and held the door open for me. "You just missed it," she whispered. "Gene repeated what he told us last night. He says he isn't worthy to take part in the play."

A white-faced Gene sat front and center, long legs dangling over the edge of the stage, head bowed in avoidance of the attention showered on him. Bobo laid his head on his lap.

"Gene was responsible for Philip Lambert's death, and Magda covered up for him?" Cord asked. Surprise and astonishment at this aberrant behavior on the part of his aunt was evident in his voice.

"Gene, as your family lawyer, I have to advise you not to say anything further." Lauren offered his legal advice.

Behind me I heard a loud thud as a bag of ice fell to the floor.

From: Jerry Burton (cbtrotter@redbud.net)
Date: Tuesday, May 6, 9:23 PM
To: Eugene Mallory (GMallory.Circle_G@ggcoc.net)
Subject: Philip Lambert

*You covered your tracks very well, but the
stench of murder clings to you.*

You will pay!

Tuesday, May 6

Peppi didn't seem to notice the ice cubes scattered across the floor. She stayed rooted in place like an ice sculpture.

"Peppi?" Dina took a step toward her. "Are you okay?"

"I'm so sorry." She sprang into action and grabbed a roll of paper towels and mopped up the mess.

"Peppi." Gene jumped down from the stage and approached her, then hesitated. "I—I don't know what to say."

"It doesn't matter." Bright red spots burned in her cheeks. "What's past is past. Now, who's going to take over the role of Abby Brewster?"

Frances sought me out. "She took that pretty well." Her whisper sounded hopeful.

I shook my head, glad for police presence at the rehearsal. The way she dropped the ice suggested only a thin lid of control kept Peppi's rage from boiling over.

"Don't worry. I came prepared," Frances reassured me. "Poor Cord isn't in much better shape than his cousin, Gene. He spent the night with a sick calf, and now he hears this."

Audie called the cast together in the vacuum following the confrontation. "I have prayed a lot about whether or not to continue this play since Magda's death. But we all know what she would say."

"The show must go on." Suzanne, dressed in casual jeans and T-shirt, looked at peace, if a little sad.

"I agree." Audie nodded at each person. "To honor her memory, we need to double our efforts to make this the best production the MGM has ever put on. And Gene, the play would not be the same without you as the doctor."

A murmur expressed the troupe's agreement.

"But what about the role of Abby Brewster? Magda was the star." Cord's voice squeaked, shock modifying its normal timbre. His shoulders slumped. He threw a dirty look at his cousin.

"About that." Audie grinned. "We have found a new talent in Grace Gulch. Enid Waldberg has graciously agreed to take over the role of Abby Brewster."

Surprised murmurs passed through the cast. I suppressed a smile. I had been the one to suggest Enid for the part. She headed Christmas and Easter plays at the church and often gave dramatic readings. I breathed a sigh of relief when her husband agreed to let her audition.

Audie and I had discussed alternates for each of the

roles in the play. Only one of his ideas surprised me. He suggested that I play the role of Elaine Harper if something happened to Peppi. Me, act in one of the plays? I laughed at the thought. Dina, or even Jenna, could pull it off better than I could.

The question of the future of the production settled, the cast started rehearsing. "It's awkward." Dina stopped by the drink table between sets and downed a glass of ice water. "Gene's acting is off tonight. I guess that's to be expected. But Peppi's a real trouper, a professional at heart."

"Don't worry about tonight," Audie advised the crew when they called it quits. "It was bound to be difficult, but it will get better. We'll meet again on Thursday."

On Wednesday Enid arrived with Suzanne at lunchtime. "Suzanne is going to meet me to go over the scene we need to rehearse tomorrow. I can't believe I agreed to do this."

Another Bible study date sidetracked, but somehow it didn't matter.

Enid protested that she couldn't act, but in my heart I knew better. Her feeble protests really said "I have to say I don't want to do it, but deep down I really do." She had already memorized her lines, delivered them well, but her nerves froze her facial expression.

"You're a natural. You only need one thing." I went to the shelf where accessories were displayed. A lace collar would give her timeless sweater an old-fashioned touch.

"I can't take this. You can't give away all your stock."

I pinned it behind her neck. "Consider it a loan, then.

If you still want to return it after the play, we'll talk about it then."

The collar did the trick. Enid Waldberg, pastor's wife, disappeared in the persona of Abby Brewster, maiden aunt and murdering spinster.

I also told Enid about the job offer at the theater in Moore and our decision.

"You're wise, my dear." Enid unclipped the collar and slipped back into her role as pastor's wife. "I'm sure you and Audie will be happy as long as you stay in the center of God's will."

Lauren addressed the assembled cast at the next rehearsal on Thursday evening. "I thought you should be the first to hear the news."

Audie and I stood to one side, our hands intertwined. I smiled at him, and he squeezed my hand. I could almost see antennae quivering on the top of Dina's head. She held a pencil over her steno pad, prepared for use during rehearsal, ready to take notes.

I studied the crowd. Frances slipped out of her seat next to Cord, presumably to go to the restroom. Enid had arrived to cheers and a chorus of "welcome." She wore the lace collar and held onto the script like a life preserver. Suzanne sat beside Gene in the front row, the two of them talking quietly. Bobo's white head poked up between their shoulders. Mayor Ron sat a few rows back, bald head bowed. Peppi had not arrived yet.

"Our director, Audwin Howe, has accepted the position as executive director of the new Grace Gulch

Center for the Arts. He will continue as managing director of the theater, of course."

"Congratulations!" Cord slapped Audie on the back, and Gene shook his hand.

Dina dove into her backpack for her camera. "Smile." She snapped a photo. "We need to save this moment for posterity." I could see her writing the photo caption in her mind. *Prominent Grace Gulch attorney, Lauren Packer, introduces Audwin Howe, the new Executive Director of the Grace Gulch Center for the Arts.*

"Speech, speech!" Suzanne led the chant.

"Quiet, please." Audie hushed the commotion with his hands. "'Memory. . .is the diary that we all carry about with us.' Wilde reminds me that the memories I have made in Grace Gulch are among my most precious possessions. Ever since I arrived in Grace Gulch, you have made me feel part of a family. I am honored to work among such fine folk."

I wiped a tear from my eye. In the end Audie said he wanted to work at the MGM because he loved Grace Gulch. He loved the people, the whole squabbling, corny lot of us. The salary that came with the executive director's job didn't hurt, either.

"While we're making announcements. . ." Suzanne stood to her feet. Her hair once again puffed high, reflecting her improved spirits. "A lot of people said horrible things about Gene last night." She motioned for him to join her, and she put an arm around his shoulder. "I've made my share of mistakes, but I know God has forgiven me, and so have you." She dropped her voice and made eye contact with everyone in her audience. "Now it's time to do the same for my brother."

Somewhere in the dark, a door creaked open.

"Mom always told me that God was ready to forgive me, whenever I could admit my sins. Well I finally listened to her, and I've made my peace with God." Gene's apology, while not as polished as Suzanne's, made as much of an impact. He straightened his shoulders. Bobo yipped his agreement. "I'm prepared to pay the price for what happened to Philip Lambert."

"That's good. Because I'm going to make sure you do." A voice called out from the side of the stage.

Peppi Lambert stood ten feet away from Gene, gun clutched in her right hand.

"You killed my father." Rage contorted Peppi's face and stiffened her arms, the gun in her right hand perfectly steady.

Gene stepped away from Suzanne. He raised his hands and walked toward Peppi, putting his body between the out-of-control woman and most of the cast. "I'm so sorry. I've. . ." His voice started to break. "I've regretted what happened every day of my life since then."

Peppi stopped a couple of feet away from Gene. I swallowed. Someone had to act before anyone got hurt. In her current mood, Peppi might shoot up the entire theater. Audie caught my eye and cocked his head to the right. I could guess his intentions.

I edged away from the circle of onlookers. Peppi swiveled in my direction. "Don't move!"

I stopped. Audie inched through the crowd. I needed to give him time to get into position. I raised my arms in the air. "It's just us folks here. You know all of us. You can tell us the truth."

"The truth. The good people of Grace Gulch wouldn't

recognize the truth if it hit them in the head. Not this town of liars and pretenders in the middle of the so-called Bible Belt. Pah." Droplets of spittle gleamed on her teeth.

"I want to know the truth." *Keep her talking.* "You thought Magda Grace Mallory killed your father. Did you know they had dated once upon a time? Your grandmother told me that."

"Those pearls. Yeah, I know the whole story. First she broke his heart and then she killed him."

Audie slid behind two more people, close to the edge of the group.

"Is that why you killed my mother?" Tears slid down Gene's cheeks, and his voice broke. "But *I* killed him. I was the one driving the car."

Peppi swung the gun wildly at Gene.

Keep quiet, I wanted to shout at him.

"As good as the same thing. She let you drive that car, and then she covered up for you. Isn't that what's called an accessory?" Peppi swept the gun in Mayor Ron's direction, where Audie had moved. "And you covered up for them."

Audie froze in place.

"Magda Grace Mallory. The grand dame of Grace Gulch. The way everybody treated her like minor royalty made me want to puke. I wanted the truth about her to come out. I figured a spot of blackmail might do the trick, but I couldn't let anybody know I was behind it."

"So you killed Vic Spencer so we'd think there were two different blackmailers, Elsie Holland and Jerry Burton." *At my store.*

"He was the perfect fall guy. I had already figured out he must be behind the burglaries across Lincoln County."

Her smug expression turned into a scowl. "You weren't supposed to figure the aliases out so quickly."

"You were both Elsie Holland and Jerry Burton."

"I thought that was a nice touch." She smirked.

"Why my store?" The question had bothered me since the murder.

"Magda's pearls, of course! The pearls that should have been mine." Peppi bit off the words. Her gun hand wavered. "The police were supposed to find the blackmail notes at the theater. They would think Magda had killed Spencer because he was blackmailing her." Her mouth settled into a grim smile, and her gun hand steadied. "She would be exposed for the murderess she was."

Audie reached the far side of the stage, out of Peppi's range of sight.

"So why did you kill Magda, then?"

"The police didn't fall for my plans. They were too interested in locating Spencer's partner. Isn't that right, Mr. Packer?"

Lauren jumped out of his seat. "I don't have to sit still for this."

"I say you do." She waved him back into his seat.

Audie finished his slow circle, only a few feet behind Peppi now.

"Magda Grace Mallory had to pay for what she did to my father. And now that I know the truth, you're going to join mother dearest." Peppi aimed her gun at Gene.

Audie lunged forward and knocked Peppi to the floor. The group scattered into the far corners of the room. I heard a side door open, but I couldn't take my eyes off the deadly wrestling match taking place in front of me.

Peppi freed her left wrist. She twisted and turned and

battled Audie for control. Her gym workouts gave her the strength of a hardened veteran.

Bang. The gun went off. The chandelier waved in the ceiling. *Bang.* A bit of plaster fell onto the seats. With a final, superhuman effort, Audie pinned Peppi to the floor and tossed the gun to the side.

I reached for the weapon. Chief Reiner interrupted me. "I'll take that." He must have entered when I heard the front door open. He bagged the weapon and strode across the floor to the loudly cursing Peppi.

"I'll take over now," Chief Reiner told Audie.

"If you don't mind. I'll stay where I am until you get the handcuffs on." The words puffed out of Audie's mouth. Sweat ran down his forehead. As soon as the handcuffs clicked around Peppi's wrist, he jumped to his feet. "Remind me to get more exercise in the future."

A small scuffle started at the front entrance. I turned in time to see Frances grab the collar of Lauren's shirt. "Not so fast, Mr. Packer." A second set of handcuffs clamped around his wrists. She began reading him his rights.

Gene remained rooted to the same place. "Do you want to take me in, too?"

The ends of Reiner's Roosevelt-style mustache quivered. "I believe I can trust you to come in later for questioning, can't I, son?" Graciousness softened the chief's tone.

Later—after Frances and another officer escorted Peppi and Lauren to the jail and Reiner questioned the witnesses—Audie and I closed up the theater and walked into the starlit night.

"I'm glad that's over." I looked up at the heavenly canopy. "'When I consider your heavens, the work of your fingers, the moon and the stars, which you have set in place, what is man that you are mindful of him, the son of man that you care for him?'"

"A contemporary psalmist might say it's just another day at the office for God. The Truth has revealed the truth about the murder."

We walked to my house. "At last the secrets have been uncovered and the mystery is solved."

"Just in time." Audie gripped my hand more tightly. "I'm glad I won't have anything more serious to worry about than two sisters who poison their guests."

I laughed. All was right with our world.

Epilogue

Saturday, June 14

Dina popped into the ladies' Sunday school classroom. "I think all of Grace Gulch has turned out for the wedding." She snapped a picture of Jenna attempting to tame my tangled hair into soft flower petals to frame my face.

My two bridesmaids looked radiant. Pale green lace covered the bodices of their satin gowns. I decided green was my favorite color, since God used so much of it in nature. Besides, the color brought out their hazel eyes.

"There is no one else I would rather share the day with." I turned in my chair and hugged them both. "The end of an era."

"And the start of another. I'll be back." Jenna spoke in her best Schwarzenegger imitation. "I can't wait for the new art center to open. But I'll save that for later. Today is your fairy tale." She patted a few curls in place and sprayed my hair lightly. "Take a look. You're glowing."

From the simple lace veil to the beaded bodice to the rose pink tulle underlying the skirt, I did look like a queen on coronation day. The time had come to set aside my detective's trench coat for a new role, the wife of the most wonderful man in the world.

Not everyone from Grace Gulch could attend the wedding. Though out on bail, Lauren Packer wouldn't dare show his face. Gene was in prison, as well. Peppi, of course, sat in the county jail awaiting trial. Dina had taken the revelations about her friend like a trouper.

"Are my girls ready?" Dad knocked at the door. "Oh, Cecilia. You remind me of your mother on our wedding day." Tears formed in his eyes, and I felt answering moisture behind my eyelids.

"Stop it, Dad. I don't want to cry and ruin my makeup." I hiccupped a laugh.

"Frances is ready to play the wedding march whenever you give the signal." Enid Waldberg would also add her musical touch, singing two solos during the service in her beautiful alto.

Dina, her hair a pale blond with only two streaks of green and pink for flair, entered first, followed by Jenna. The music swelled.

I nodded at Dad, and we walked through the open door.

My future waited at the altar.

Award-winning author and speaker Darlene Franklin resides in the Colorado foothills with her mother and her lynx point Siamese cat Talia. One daughter has preceded her into glory; Darlene's son and his family live in Oklahoma. She loves music, needlework, reading, and reality TV. She has published two books and one novella with Barbour: *Romanian Rhapsody, Gunfight at Grace Gulch* (book one in the Dressed for Death series), and *Dressed in Scarlet* (featured in the Christmas anthology, *Snowbound Colorado Christmas*). Visit Darlene's blog at www.darlenefranklinwrites.blogspot.com or her Web site at www.darlenehfranklin.com.

You may correspond with this author by writing:
Darlene Franklin
Author Relations
PO Box 721
Uhrichsville, OH 44683

A Letter to Our Readers

Dear Reader:

In order to help us satisfy your quest for more great mystery stories, we would appreciate it if you would take a few minutes to respond to the following questions. We welcome your comments and read each form and letter we receive. When completed, please return to:

Fiction Editor
Heartsong Presents—MYSTERIES!
PO Box 721
Uhrichsville, Ohio 44683

Did you enjoy reading *A String of Murders* by Darlene Franklin?

☉ Very much! I would like to see more books like this! The one thing I particularly enjoyed about this story was:

_____
_____
_____

☉ Moderately. I would have enjoyed it more if:

_____
_____
_____

Are you a member of the HP—MYSTERIES! Book Club?
☉ Yes ☉ No

If no, where did you purchase this book?

_____

Please rate the following elements using a scale of 1 (poor) to 10 (superior):

___ Main character/sleuth   ___ Romance elements

___ Inspirational theme   ___ Secondary characters

___ Setting   ___ Mystery plot

How would you rate the cover design on a scale of 1 (poor) to 5 (superior)? _____

What themes/settings would you like to see in future **Heartsong Presents—MYSTERIES!** selections? _____
_____
_____
_____

Please check your age range:
     ○ Under 18   ○ 18–24
     ○ 25–34   ○ 35–45
     ○ 46–55   ○ Over 55

Name: _____

Occupation: _____

Address: _____

E-mail address: _____